MOUNTAIN GIRL, RIVER GIRL

TING-XING YE, born in Shanghai in 1952, was an English interpreter for the Chinese government before leaving China in 1987. Her memoir, *A Leaf in the Bitter Wind,* has been published in nine countries. She is also the author of *Throwaway Daughter* and the award-winning *White Lily.* She lives in Orillia, Ontario.

Also by Ting-xing Ye

A Leaf in the Bitter Wind

My Name Is Number Four

Throwaway Daughter

White Lily

Three Monks, No Water

Weighing the Elephant

Share the Sky

山妹子

Mountain Girl, River Girl

a novel

水妹子

Ting-xing Ye

PUFFIN CANADA

PUFFIN CANADA

Published by the Penguin Group

Penguin Group (Canada), 90 Eglinton Avenue East, Suite 700, Toronto, Ontario, Canada M4P 2Y3 (a division of Pearson Canada Inc.)
Penguin Group (USA) Inc., 375 Hudson Street, New York, New York 10014, U.S.A.
Penguin Books Ltd, 80 Strand, London WC2R 0RL, England
Penguin Ireland, 25 St Stephen's Green, Dublin 2, Ireland (a division of Penguin Books Ltd)
Penguin Group (Australia), 250 Camberwell Road, Camberwell, Victoria 3124, Australia (a division of Pearson Australia Group Pty Ltd)
Penguin Books India Pvt Ltd, 11 Community Centre, Panchsheel Park, New Delhi – 110 017, India
Penguin Group (NZ), 67 Apollo Drive, Rosedale, North Shore 0632, New Zealand (a division of Pearson New Zealand Ltd)
Penguin Books (South Africa) (Pty) Ltd, 24 Sturdee Avenue, Rosebank, Johannesburg 2196, South Africa

Penguin Books Ltd, Registered Offices: 80 Strand, London WC2R 0RL, England

First published 2008

1 2 3 4 5 6 7 8 9 10 (WEB)

Publisher's note: This book is a work of fiction. Names, characters, places and incidents either are the product of the author's imagination or are used fictitiously, and any resemblance to actual persons living or dead, events, or locales is entirely coincidental.

Manufactured in Canada.

ISBN-13: 978-0-14-316812-6
ISBN-10: 0-14-316812-6

LIBRARY AND ARCHIVES CANADA CATALOGUING IN PUBLICATION

Ye, Ting-xing, 1952–
Mountain girl, river girl / Ting-xing Ye.

ISBN 978-0-14-316812-6

1. China—Social conditions—21st century—Juvenile fiction.
2. Rural-urban migration—China—Juvenile fiction. I. Title.

PS8597.E16M69 2008 jC813'.54 C2007-905660-1

A Note on Pronunciation and Usage

The standard pin-yin notation is used throughout. Most letters in pin-yin are pronounced more or less the same as in English.

Pan-pan is pronounced as in English.

Shui-lian is pronounced "shway lee-an."

The words Lao (old, venerable) and Xiao (young) when used with a surname are common terms of respect in China.

For Bill, who calls China his second home.

柳暗花明又一村
山重水复疑无路

Shan chong shui fu yi wu lu
Liu an hua ming you yi cun

Mountain folds into mountain,
river flows into river,
with no path in sight.
In the shadow of a willow
wildflowers glow.
A village comes in view.

—FROM "TOURING SHANXI VILLAGE"
BY SONG DYNASTY POET LU YOU, 1125–1210

山水相连

Part One

Shan shui xiang lian

Where there is a mountain,
there is a river.

Chapter One

Pan-pan

"Give the back of your neck a good scrub."

Startled, her heart pounding in her throat, Pan-pan gripped the rim of the enamel washbasin to contain her irritation. "Yes, Ah-Po," she murmured.

"And behind your ears."

"Yes, Ah-Po."

"Good Heavens! They're a whole shade darker than the rest of your skin," the old woman rattled on. "You should know they're also part of your face."

"Are they really?" Pan-pan muttered, slowly turning away from the stone sink. Blinking and squeezing soapy water out of her eyes, she looked up to find that the tip of her nose was only an inch away from her grandmother's.

"Yes, Ah-Po," she said again.

"And—"

"And," Pan-pan cut her off, lifting her chin and staring into her grandmother's eyes, "give my armpits a good wash and dust them with the talcum powder *you* so kindly bought for me."

"*Aiya,* Pan-er," Ah-Po exclaimed, her voice rising. "Did you eat gunpowder for supper last night? Fine, then. Do whatever you want! I'm leaving. Why do I care so much?" she lamented, reaching to brush soapy water off Pan-pan's bare shoulder with her open palm before she turned and shuffled toward the door. There she raised her plump arms in surrender and called out, "I give up. It's your face, after all. And your body."

"You'll never give up!" Pan-pan shot back angrily, but not until the kitchen door had shut behind her grandmother. "As for today, *my* face and *my* body are all yours." She paused, making sure that Ah-Po was gone, and yelled, "And don't call me Pan-er. I'm not a boy. My name is Pan-pan!"

Pan-pan had told Ah-Po time after time that she didn't like to be sneaked up on, particularly when she was washing herself. That was why for months she had been getting up each morning before anyone else in the house. Now, two weeks before her fifteenth birthday, Pan-pan enjoyed having the tiny kitchen to herself. She cherished the quiet moments and solitude, or her "privacy," a word she had heard Xin-Ma—new mother—use a lot lately.

Rubbing her neck with a rough cloth, Pan-pan held back another surge of fury as she realized that even the hinges on the door had betrayed her, letting her grandmother come into the kitchen unheard. For as long as she could remember, the warped wooden door had squeaked each time it was pushed open. Didn't Mom use to say that when a person is feeling low or struck by bad luck, she can be bullied by her own shadow?

Thinking about her mother brought tears to Pan-pan's eyes, and, overcome with frustration, she wiped them away with the back of her hand more forcefully than necessary. Today's grand ceremony would mark the third anniversary of Mom's death. Her father had remarried, and over a year ago Xin-Ma had given birth to Gui-yang, Pan-pan's half-brother. No matter how hard she tried, Pan-pan couldn't work up much enthusiasm for the coming rituals.

No one in the family had ever explained to Pan-pan why her mother had died so unexpectedly at the age of thirty-six. People are not supposed to die so young, and Mom hadn't even been sick. Many times Pan-pan had begged her father for an answer, but each time he hemmed and hawed as if he had suddenly lost his voice. He would fidget, rubbing the back of his neck or repeatedly wiping his face with his hand. His pain and agony were so hard to watch that eventually Pan-pan stopped asking him questions altogether.

Trying to get information out of Ah-Po posed a different challenge; she simply ignored Pan-pan, playing deaf and dumb, using her favourite evasion, "I'm an old bag of bones who should be treated with respect, not pestered with questions." Pan-pan had concluded long ago that it would be easier to find a three-legged chicken than the truth about her own mother's death.

Pan-pan could still vividly recall the morning she and her father had seen Mom off at the local donkey-cart depot. Mom planned to ride the cart to the long-distance bus station and board the bus for the fifty-kilometre trip northwest to the city of Tongren, where Auntie Cai-fei, Mom's older sister, lived with her family.

It was an unusually cold spring morning and Mom had insisted Pan-pan wear the wool hat that Ah-Po had knitted for her. Mom promised Pan-pan she was going to buy her the best birthday present anyone in the village had ever seen. "That's why I have to go alone," she had said mysteriously, "or the gift won't be a surprise."

"It's not fair," Pan-pan had whined, plucking at her hat. "First you won't take me, now you want me to look like a turtle. Why do I have to cover my hair? I want to look like you," she added, pointing to her mom's new perm. Earlier that morning Ah-Po had remarked that Mom's short and curly hair resembled a duck's behind.

"It's a new millennium next year, dear Po-Po," Mom had responded, smiling happily and showing the dimples at the corners of her mouth. "Catch up with the trend, will you?"

It was Dad who had insisted that he and Pan-pan walk Mom all the way to the depot in the neighbouring village, despite Mom's objection that it was too far for Pan-pan and the mountain road too winding and steep. Pan-pan knew what she meant. The road was called the "Trail of Sheep's Intestines" because of its many twists and turns, abrupt rises and perilous descents, and its narrow, uneven surface. As the three of them slowly made their way, Mom chatted and laughed with Pan-pan, but Dad stayed quiet most of the time, trudging ahead of them with Mom's woven bamboo basket, heavy with dried beans, dates, and sunflower seeds for Auntie Cai-fei's family, strapped to his back.

At the depot, before climbing into the wagon pulled by a donkey, Mom had thrown her arms around Dad and pressed her lips against his. Dad blushed, amid the laughter of farmers waiting for a ride. But he'd smiled for the first time since they left home. Mom then took Pan-pan in her arms and kissed her on her forehead. As the cart rumbled away, she called out again that she would bring back a wonderful gift for Pan-pan's twelfth birthday.

That was the last time Pan-pan saw her mother laugh. A week later she was brought home on a stretcher. There was no birthday present. Ten days later, her mother died.

In the days following her mother's death, Pan-pan lay on her back on the bed she shared with Ah-Po, staring at the criss-crossed bamboo poles that supported the thatched roof. From time to time, her eyes were drawn to the corner of the room where, on top of the chest of drawers, her mother's picture stood, now wrapped in black ribbons. Pan-pan found no peace anywhere she looked, particularly at night. Each time she closed her eyes and drifted off to sleep, she was startled awake by the sound of her own sobbing. She wondered if she would ever be able to sleep again.

"Are you still awake?" Ah-Po's voice rose beside her one night. "Be strong my child," she added softly, almost pleading.

"Yes, Ah-Po," said Pan-pan, drying her tears before she turned onto her side. Ah-Po's words reminded her of the happy years when she was doted on by three grown-ups and enjoyed an endless share of their love and care. It was when she earned her reputation as a strong-willed child, or to use her teacher's words, someone with a "high tolerance for pain." Mom had laughed good-naturedly at the comment. During a school outing, on a narrow path in the mountains, Pan-pan had badly scraped both knees as she held onto the harness of a sliding donkey that had lost its footing. The blood had oozed through her pant legs, yet she hadn't uttered one complaint until the donkey was safely pulled back up the slope. Ah-Po ought to know that there was a big difference between losing some blood and losing one's mother, Pan-pan thought as she lay in the dark. She worried that with Mom forever gone, she'd never be strong again.

Now, three years later, Pan-pan couldn't remember the details of the funeral, the burial of her mother's ashes, or the disappearance of her father. And she recalled only vaguely his turning up a few days later in the back of a police car, smelly and drunk, his hands wrapped in dirty bandages. He had stumbled into the house with Ah-Po's sharp words ringing in his ears.

Shortly after his hands had healed, Dad decided to follow the lead of other villagers and quit the life of a farmer. Taking with him a small bag and a bedroll, he headed out to the cities to take on jobs that urban dwellers declined to do.

How ironic it is, Pan-pan thought bitterly as she carefully powdered her armpits and buttoned up her shirt. Mom had once told her that she and Dad had named her Pan-pan—Hope—because they wanted their daughter to be free to wish for anything she liked. Yet Pan-pan couldn't even find the answer to the question that had plagued her for the past three years—Why had her mother been taken from her so suddenly? It was obvious that something unexpected, even horrible, had happened in Tongren, but no one would tell her what it was.

Her parents, Pan-pan thought, should have called her Hopeless.

Chapter Two

Shui-lian

The rain came first, then fog swept in before darkness descended on the bay like a lid on a wok. At the bow of her family's riverboat, which was tied alongside a jetty, Shui-lian stood stretching her legs, numb from squatting on her heels. She tossed the dishwater into the river and gazed into the distance toward the city's main wharf, where, once again, a cluster of giant boats was moored, as if floating on top of one another. All were wider, longer, and taller than the sheds and warehouses that huddled along the bank. The area was so brightly lit that the glare seemed to have burned a large hole in the thick mist, illuminating the starless sky and coating the surrounding water with a golden finish. Cruise ships, they are called, not boats, Shui-lian reminded herself as a file of buses pulled up to the quay, like fish swimming upriver.

Spring was well under way in this part of the country and so was the popular cruise down the Long River, or the Yangtze, as it was called by the foreign tourists, whose glamour and lavish behaviour had once again turned Chongqing, City of Fog, into a sleepless port. The daily voyages customarily took off at the crack of dawn, leaving the locals to wake up to an abandoned dock.

Standing on the scarred wooden deck, Shui-lian tried to imagine what it would be like to sleep inside such grand and spacious vessels. Yet she found it equally difficult to understand the appeal of floating on water, something she had been doing since she had come into this world—a curse she was about to end once and for all in a matter of hours. *Zai-jian*—see you again—she whispered to the inky water before she walked back to the small cabin. "What's wrong with you!" she grumbled, slapping the side of her head with annoyance. "No. I don't want to see this river ever again."

Early next morning Shui-lian quietly slipped off her canvas cot. She tiptoed past the raised platform where her mother lay snoring softly beside Shui-lian's younger sister and out onto the deck. The air was like a damp, heavy blanket cast over the bay. She paused to listen, her eyes on the tiny wheelhouse at the stern where her older brother, Shui-shen, slept with his new bride. Holding her shoes in one hand and a small shoulder bag in another, she crept down the gangplank. The boards of the jetty felt slippery and cool against her bare soles. Inside her bag was a plastic pouch containing fifty yuan and some coins—all her savings—and a pair of new socks, the kind that stretched nicely to fit. Even though she couldn't remember the last time she had worn socks, she was clearly aware of the significance of putting them on for the big event ahead. No one would laugh at her the way Shui-shen had when he caught her trying them on.

"Light a candle for a blind man," he'd chuckled. "We are boat people. Socks to us are like giving a comb to a monk."

At one time, Shui-lian would have shut her older brother up quickly before he drew another breath. "Who died and went to

Western Heaven and left you in charge?" she would snap, using one of her favourite expressions. It wasn't just her words that silenced her brother or anyone else who tried to put her down but the way her lips curled up at the corner and her eyes flared like wildfire. Her mother had long declared that Shui-lian's tongue and manner were like the local cuisine, so spicy and peppery it left diners speechless by the end of a meal. Shui-lian had admitted to her friend Jin-lin that the first time she spat out the words she had no idea what they meant, not even the reference to Western Heaven. She had overheard bickering boaters say it and liked the sound of it. The times she used it were among the few occasions she was able to make herself noticed. "Little Sichuan," her mother called her because of her feisty and quick temper—the province of Sichuan being famously mutinous: "The first to rebel and the last to submit."

Shui-lian's father had been a river *ku-li*—coolie—like his father, and his father's father. She too had been born on a boat and raised on the water. For generations, her family had made their living by pulling cargo boats on the four rivers that gave Sichuan its name. From the day she was able to sit up on her own, Shui-lian had watched her father up ahead on the riverbanks, sometimes with other men, hauling a row of boats loaded with coal, grain, logs, or bags of cement and other material through the surging water. With thick ropes made of hemp taut across his shoulders, her father leaned head down into the strain, bent double, pushing into the sun, fog, wind, and storm, passing through gorges and scuffling on rock-strewn banks. Guiding the boats downstream was equally difficult and dangerous. Each step was an agony and every trip a misery. Both her father and brother had leathery calluses on the soles of their feet and fearsome scars on their backs.

Three years ago, when Shui-lian was twelve, she watched, horrified, as her father lost his footing on the slippery clay of a towpath, fell into the Jialing River, and was quickly swept away by the turbulent green water. His body was never found. From time to time Shui-lian couldn't help but wonder superstitiously if her mouthiness had tempted the river devils to bring about her father's early death, leaving her mother a widow and her brother head of the family. She had tried to make up for her wrongs, offering to help her brother, yet each time she went near the stout rope her brother used for towing someone yelled at her. Tradition asserted that the mere touch of a female hand on the rope would cause the boats to capsize and sink, and bring bad luck to the family.

"How can our luck be any worse than losing a father?" Shui-lian would snap back in frustration, only to be boxed on the ears by her mother for insolence.

With four mouths to feed, her mother and brother had been trying for several months to marry her off to a boatman. Shui-lian had refused. Even if the man were not fifteen years older than her and as ugly as a carp, she wouldn't have agreed. Her mind had been made up, long before her father's death. If she ever did marry, her husband must have a piece of land for her to stand on and a place to bury her ashes when she died.

But her mother would not listen. "He owns two boats," she pointed out. "He has some money, and he's willing to take you without a dowry. Get those nonsense dreams out of your head once and for all. You're a river girl, and seven months from now, once you turn sixteen, whether you like or not, you'll be a river wife!"

So the previous morning, when Jin-lin had come to tell Shui-lian about the recruiting team, Shui-lian decided it was her only chance to escape. What choice do I have? she asked herself. Married or single, I'll still live on a boat for the rest of my life.

"I heard it'll be at Sandbar Village tomorrow," Jin-lin whispered to her as they sat beneath the awning of her family's boat, eating rice porridge. "They're looking for young women to work in clothing factories in Shanghai."

"Factory? Shanghai?" Shui-lian exclaimed, her eyes brightening.

"Yes," Jin-lin giggled, revealing a toothy smile. "Can you imagine? Not only will we earn a salary and have our own money, we'll be surrounded by tall buildings, instead of mountains, and wide asphalt boulevards, not endless waterways. Everyone there is rich and beautiful, and even the air is scented! Better still," she paused to take a mouthful of air before continuing, "because the water level is unusually low this spring, the cargo freighters can't enter Chongqing harbour, which means our boats will be stranded here for a few more days, which also means that you and I can easily slip away without much notice and fuss. We've got to be at Sandbar Village before everyone else. I don't want to miss the boat."

"Neither do I," said Shui-lian, looking over the rim of her rice bowl at Jin-lin, wondering if her friend had made the pun on purpose.

Jin-lin was eighteen, three years older than Shui-lian. They had met as young girls at a "floating school" created for families of fishers and boat *ku-lis* as part of the government campaign to eliminate illiteracy. The school had been set up on a cement barge that moved from one dock to another, thus earning its name. The square-bowed vessel had an open, flat deck on which rows of small desks were placed, with low stools behind them. A blackboard hung on the wall of the engine cabin. The pupils had a different teacher each trip, depending on whether the boat travelled upstream or down, and he or she welcomed anyone who was willing to learn to read, write, and do math. It was a fair-weather operation, as it turned out. There was no school if it rained, no classes when the temperature dropped too low or soared too high. Yet on fine days, few students showed up because most were needed by their families as extra hands. Bored most of the time by the monotonous drills in Chinese and arithmetic, Shui-lian didn't mind missing classes.

"It reminds me of the lyric about a lazy fisher," Shui-lian once joked, "who goes out fishing for two days and stays at home to mend his net for the rest of the week." Her remark didn't sit well with her classmates, who were either fishers themselves or the children of fishers.

After two years, Shui-lian and Jin-lin had stopped going to the school but remained friends, managing to see each other whenever their boats anchored at the same port. At those times they were as inseparable as a body and its shadow.

Jin-lin's problem at home, she confided to Shui-lian as they ate, wasn't that her parents wanted to find her a husband. "It's my father. He's been attempting to get wifely duties from me ever since my mother became ill after giving birth to another baby girl."

"He *what*?" Shui-lian exclaimed, her chopsticks frozen in midair.

"Keep your voice down. I don't want to cause any trouble for my family," Jin-lin whispered.

"Does your mother know about this?" Shui-lian hissed.

"I'm not sure. If she does, she's never said one word about it, at least not to me," Jin-lin answered, shaking her head. "But I know he won't give up until he gets what he wants," she said sadly, gazing at the raindrops as they hit the water, creating ripple after ripple. "Where is the iron fist of the government when you really need it?" she grumbled, spitting into the water and startling a team of ducks paddling near the riverbank.

"The government is more interested in enforcing its one-child-per-family policy. It should be protecting people like you!" Shui-lian said angrily.

"You're right. But it's not very successful, is it? Look at my family, three girls already, and still no end to it." Jin-lin laughed bitterly. "All I can do is to leave, put these troubles behind and start a new life in Shanghai or some other city."

Like many of the river people, Shui-lian had never set foot in a big city, not even Chengdu, Sichuan's capital. She'd seen it many times in the distance, when her family boat passed the city's waterfront, and lately tall buildings had appeared, replacing the old houses. There was talk about reforms and progress, new words she'd heard more and more in the wharf markets around

Sichuan. There she'd also learned that travelling from place to place was allowed, that private ownership was encouraged, and that foreigners, once driven out of the country, had returned to the government's open-armed welcome. The latest gossip was that hundreds of thousands of peasants were heading toward urban areas to earn ready cash, leaving behind their families, unplanted seeds, and farmland. The most capable had made their way to China's coveted coastal cities, like Shanghai and Guangzhou. Shui-lian often wondered what it would be like to visit such places—or even live there, with dry land under her feet.

"One thing is sure," Jin-lin said as she slurped up the last of her porridge, "if we stay here any longer, we'll end up living the life of our mothers, and we'll never get the rotten river smell off our skin. We must grab this chance to get out."

And now, only one day later, Shui-lian was doing just that. She turned her back on the river and ran toward the spot where she and Jin-lin had planned to meet.

Chapter Three

Pan-pan

Pan-pan stood before the brick stove, which took up half of the kitchen, waiting for the millet porridge to boil in the big iron wok. Gazing out the window at the mountains to the north that tumbled away into purple distance, she wondered what lay beyond. No matter what, she assured herself as she stirred the porridge, it must be more exciting and adventurous than life in this rocky village.

"*Lai-le, lai-le*—It's coming! It's coming!"

Pan-pan's thought was cut off by the chatter of animated voices and pounding footsteps on the path outside the house. She looked up and saw a group of children scurrying past the window like frightened ducks. A slow-moving tractor, snorting puffs of smoke into the crispy morning air, seemed to be chasing them. In the wagon hitched to the tractor a dozen black-robed men sat serenely, their shaved heads reflecting the pale sunlight like mirrors, their sandalled feet dangling over the wagon's edge.

"Dad," Pan-pan called out, "the monks are here."

"It's a good omen. They're here on time." Her stepmother, holding Gui-yang on one hip, rushed into the kitchen. "Look, Pan-pan," Xin-Ma cried out, her free hand pointing out the window and up at the hill. "The truck! The house! Oh my goodness, everything has arrived at once!"

Pan-pan dropped her wooden spoon and removed the pot from the burner. Craning her neck, she could see an old blue truck slowly picking its way down the steep, bumpy road that led to her village, horn blaring, brakes screeching and panting. When the vehicle made a tight turn, it revealed a nearly full-size house made of paper pasted over a bamboo stick frame, with a black roof and gold-coloured walls.

"It even has a chimney!" Xin-Ma exclaimed, shifting her son to the other hip.

When the truck finally clattered past the kitchen window, Pan-pan found herself eye to eye with one of three chickens standing in front of double vermilion doors. The stiff, glass-eyed birds—but with real feathers—were going nowhere. Their golden feet were glued onto a large green piece of cardboard.

"Your mother was a very lucky woman," Xin-Ma murmured, sounding almost envious. "All this cost your father a fortune. The monks, the ceremony, and of course this grand paper house and everything in it," she continued, without looking at Pan-pan, "all the money he's saved from hauling rocks down from the mountain on his back."

"I know," Pan-pan answered, moving away from the window and picking up the spoon. Yet she wondered, as she ladled the gruel into a large bowl and set it on the stove, how Xin-Ma could talk about death and luck in one breath. Oh, she means well, Pan-pan told herself, she's just trying to cheer me up.

"Breakfast is ready," Pan-pan announced.

PAN-PAN'S FATHER had met Xin-Ma in Guiyang, the capital of Guizhou Province, at a highway construction site. By then he'd been working there for six months, along with thousands of other men and women, building a "freeway," as he called it, using the English word. "Three lanes each way," he'd said to Ah-Po and Pan-pan during his first visit home. "And when it's completed, the motor cars will be able to go the speed of a bullet—at least one hundred kilometres an hour!"

Pan-pan had little concept of a hundred kilometres. In her mountain village, Yunxi—Western Clouds—all the houses were built on various levels of a slope. The terraced fields were hand-dug into the shoulders of hills. Their narrow widths and irregular lengths were measured in *chi*—a third of a metre—and in metres. According to a local folk song, each road turned behind a hill every three metres and a sunny sky never lasted more than three days.

Xin-Ma's home village had been in the path of the new freeway, so when the government order came for a new road to be put through, all the inhabitants were relocated, scattered like sand across the province. Many, like Xin-Ma, tempted by steady cash wages and freedom from field work, had been hired as unskilled labourers, lugging stones on their backs in bamboo baskets or, as in Xin-Ma's case, breaking up large rocks with a sledgehammer.

Ah-Po blamed Xin-Ma for tarnishing her family's reputation by marrying her widowed son and thereby breaking the local tradition of a three-year mourning period. "We're bound to be punished," she had repeatedly predicted when Pan-pan's father brought Xin-Ma home for the New Year's celebration only one year after the death of his first wife. Ever since, nothing about Xin-Ma would satisfy Ah-Po: not the way she walked, sat, or talked. "Too saucy, too shrieky," the old woman constantly complained, grinding the few teeth she had left. "And too blunt."

"This is the voice I was born with," Xin-Ma would say behind Ah-Po's back, stamping her foot. "And I'm not blunt. I'm straightforward. It just happens that my guts have fewer twists than others," meaning that she wasn't phoney.

It wasn't the broken tradition that saddened Pan-pan. She didn't want a new mother. Who did this stranger with the high-pitched voice—Ah-Po was right about that!—think she was, marching into Pan-pan's home and into her life, as though she owned both?

After the New Year's visit, Dad had returned to the construction site, leaving Xin-Ma with Pan-pan and her grandmother. Seven months later, along came Pan-pan's half-brother, Gui-yang—Precious Sunshine—named after the provincial capital. On the day Gui-yang was born, Ah-Po ceased bickering and whining about her new daughter-in-law. She even started to tell her neighbours and anyone else who would listen that the arrival of a grandson was the result of her persistence in calling her granddaughter "Pan-er"—Hope for a son. "It worked," she crowed. "It paid off!"

"I gave birth to this boy," Xin-Ma would say, lifting her chin, her eyes flashing. "It's all my doing, damn it, not hers." She would then turn to Pan-pan. "I suppose if the old woman kept calling you 'Empress Dowager' you'd someday become an emperor's mother!"

Pan-pan hated being dragged into a fight she had nothing to do with. And she was equally annoyed at being compared to the infamous Empress Dowager, who, according to the stories Pan-pan had heard, was as evil and ugly as a poisonous snake. Worse, the nasty empress had been dead for over a hundred years. Everyone knew that comparing the living to the dead would bring bad luck. No wonder Ah-Po said Xin-Ma should hire a soldier to guard her mouth.

Eventually, Pan-pan's bitterness toward Xin-Ma, or *hou-niang*—later mother—as the villagers called her, faded. Xin-Ma was all right, Pan-pan admitted, even kind and generous, but as long as Pan-pan lived she would never refer to Xin-Ma as good. That would be betraying her own mother. At the same time, Pan-pan realized she would never again feel completely secure and at ease in her own home, the way she'd felt when her mother was alive. Now the family was Ah-Po, Dad, Xin-Ma, and Gui-yang—and Pan-pan was an add-on, more like a temporary guest than a daughter.

Xin-Ma, meanwhile, had told Pan-pan over and over that she was fond of her, and assured her that so long as Pan-pan didn't cause her any trouble, they would get along just fine. Once, she'd even suggested that if it would make Pan-pan feel better, Pan-pan could call her Jie-Jie—Elder Sister—instead. "Let's face it," said Xin-Ma with a ringing giggle, "I'm only twelve years older than you, which means we both were born in the year of the rabbit. In other words, we face the same fate."

In the past two years they had gotten along well, just as Xin-Ma had predicted, even after Pan-pan confided to her that no matter how nicely she treated Pan-pan, she could never replace her real mother. Xin-Ma had frowned but then shrugged, saying she understood. Nevertheless, in the days after the wedding, there had been no shortage of people in the village who seemed to enjoy telling Pan-pan tales of cruel stepmothers, some even calling up legends from the time before Emperor Qin reunited China. How badly those wicked women mistreated the children who were not their own! How evil and ferocious they were! "Better to live with a widowed mother who's a beggar than with a remarried father who is rich and holds a high position," a couple of elders had recited to Pan-pan, quoting an old expression, shaking their heads sadly.

Yet it was Xin-Ma herself who had related to Pan-pan a strange story of an evil stepmother. She claimed that she had heard it at the construction site before she met Pan-pan's father. "I might have missed a few bits here and there," she warned Pan-pan before beginning the tale of how an unlucky girl who had lost her mother was mistreated by her stepmother and jealous older stepsisters. The girl was forced to cook and clean the house all day and was given only leftovers to eat and hand-me-downs to wear. "Yet somehow," Xin-Ma stopped, scratching her head and peering up at the ceiling as if that would help her recall more details, "somehow one day she was asked to try on a pair of glass shoes."

"Are you sure that's what they were made of? Glass?"

"Certainly, young lady," Xin-Ma asserted, letting Pan-pan know that she didn't appreciate being interrupted, let alone questioned. "Never mind. I for one would call it a mean trick. And cruel. How could the poor child walk in glass shoes? Or dance?"

"Dance?" Pan-pan interrupted again.

"Now what?"

"Why would the girl want to dance? She must have been heartbroken, with her mother dead and mean women to live with. Sad people don't dance—or sing."

"How on earth do I know?" Xin-Ma sniffed loudly. "Does it matter? Why do you have to question every detail? It's a story. A tale. The girl put the glass shoes on and went out dancing, and met a prince. End of story. On the other hand," she paused, letting her words linger, "if the poor child had refused to try on the glass shoes, she'd probably still be at home cleaning and cooking instead of marrying a charming prince and living happily ever after in a big palace with lots of servants and," she paused again, laughing, "giving birth to a boy named Sunshine!"

"You made up that last part!" Pan-pan protested, smiling despite herself. "I guess you're right. If the girl hadn't gone out, her life wouldn't have changed. Maybe leaving home and looking for adventure isn't a bad idea. I've been wondering myself whether I should give it a try, like Dad and some of the other villagers."

"Listen, stop talking nonsense." Xin-Ma was serious now. "All I'm saying is that you don't have to worry about me mistreating you. That's my point. There's nothing to gain for me. I'm happy for what I have now. A son of my own, a husband who loves me, a roof over my head, and plenty food on the table. And, of course, you," she quickly added, pinching Pan-pan's cheek. "You're a pretty girl. Your skin is so pale and smooth. To tell you the truth, I wouldn't mind having a girl child myself. Since your father is a

Miao, I could, couldn't I? The government allows minority families to have a second child. Your mother could have."

But Pan-pan knew that her mother hadn't wanted a second child, boy or girl. She'd overheard an argument between her parents late one night when they thought Pan-pan was asleep in the next room. Her mother's voice, usually soft and gentle, was tense and harsh. Her father spoke quietly, almost pleading, but insistently. Auntie Cai-fei was mentioned a couple of times. Pan-pan had to strain to hear her father's words.

"I wish you'd told me you've been unhappy about this all these years. But—"

"No buts this time, Dao-feng. I never tried to hide my feelings from you, you know that. This is different. It's just that times have changed, and now I may have a chance to do something about my problem. Trust me, I've thought about it long and hard, back and forth, over and over. And I've decided to go ahead, to get it done. To end it once and for all. So please don't try to stop me."

"Lin-fei, I don't care what other people think or say, if that's what bothers you. You should know that by now. I've been in love with you ever since we were kids. As soon as we were old enough I asked you to marry me. Nothing, and I mean absolutely nothing in this world, will change how I feel about you. I—"

"Oh, you stop it. Your charm won't work this time," Mom had cut him off. "I've made up my mind. Nothing can change my decision, not even the strength of nine water buffaloes yoked together."

"Would having another baby help?" Dad asked. "Isn't it about time Pan-pan had a little brother or sister to play with?"

"You just don't get it, do you?" Mom began to cry bitterly, her voice rising. "Damn it! I don't want another baby! I won't take the risk of having another imperfect child. I couldn't stand more humiliation."

Pan-pan gasped. Her stomach dropped, her heart hammered in her ears. Mom's talking about me! she thought. But what's wrong with me? What did she mean by *humiliation*?

Pan-pan was so shocked and confused she didn't notice that her grandmother beside her had stopped snoring. Ah-Po rose from their bed and stomped out of the room.

"If you don't pity an old bag of bones, at least show some mercy on your child. We're trying to sleep!" Ah-Po scolded.

The next morning, all three adults got up at the usual time and went about their routines as though what had happened just hours earlier was no more than Pan-pan's bad dream. But it hadn't been a dream. She had clearly heard her mother say that there was something wrong with Pan-pan. "Imperfect" was the word she used. The flaw went so deep that Mom didn't want more children. The hurt that Pan-pan felt was so powerful it drove her to silence for a couple of days. When finally she resolved to confront her mother and beg for an explanation, she never got the chance. A week later, Mom told Pan-pan she was going to Tongren to visit Auntie Cai-fei—alone.

"Don't look so worried, Pan-pan," she said cheerfully. "I'll be back before you know I'm gone."

Chapter Four

Shui-lian

Finally the drizzle stopped, yet the sky remained laden with thick grey clouds threatening another downpour. Shui-lian leaned against the trunk of a willow tree a few metres off the road, waiting for Jin-lin to show up. She put on her socks and clenched her teeth tight, shivering inside her thin cotton jacket and wishing that she'd brought her woollen sweater with her, the one her mother had knitted for her fifteenth birthday five months earlier. The heavy pullover was warm and soft against her skin, and it was fire red, her favourite colour. But shortly after the Spring Festival, the Lunar New Year celebration, her mother had stored the sweater away for the next year. Now it was lying at the bottom of a large wooden box, with a handful of mothballs.

At last, Shui-lian caught sight of Jin-lin, fussing over her hair as she hurried up the dirt road.

Shui-lian stood up. "Finally!" she said with annoyance. "Let's go!"

"Yes, let's!" Jin-lin smiled, her eyes shining.

An hour passed before they reached Sandbar Village, where the recruiters were conducting their job interviews. If Shui-lian had expected to see a large crowd, with drums beating and gongs clanging, she was disappointed, but at the same time relieved. They must have got there before anyone else, she told herself. Everywhere she looked, doors were closed, windows shut tight, and silence prevailed. The only creatures up and moving were some chickens, pecking aimlessly as they strutted along a footpath of hard-packed soil. There was no sign at all of a recruiting team. Nevertheless, Shui-lian and Jin-lin began to search up and down the narrow laneways and between the rows of houses. But the place turned out to be a maze. Three times they found themselves back where they'd started.

Finally they spotted a group of women gathered in front of a one-storey building at the end of a twisty alley. Like most of the houses they'd seen, this one had a blackened straw roof and whitewashed mud walls fading to yellow. So much for an early start, Shui-lian grumbled. She grabbed Jin-lin by the sleeve and pulled her toward the group. The women waiting in line looked older than Shui-lian and were dressed more stylishly. Most wore brightly coloured jackets with shiny buttons that reflected the morning sunlight every time they moved. A couple of them even sported new perms. Shui-lian wished she'd spent some time fixing her own hair. Who's going to hire a ragged thing like me, she thought, when there are better dressed and more mature women to choose from? Her courage failed her, and she cast an angry glance at Jin-lin, as though blaming her friend for not warning her.

Jin-lin merely shrugged and smiled sheepishly. "We might as well join the lineup, now that we're here."

As the morning dragged on, more women trickled into the line. Shui-lian was hungry and nervous, but most of her discomfort stemmed from her feet. They were hot in her new socks and, worse, they had swelled, her toes now squeezing against each other inside her rubber shoes. By the time the door finally opened, there were nearly twenty young women waiting. A few chatted nosily. The rest remained silent, like Shui-lian and Jin-lin, holding back their anxiety and curiosity.

Shui-lian craned her neck and stood on tiptoe, peering through the gaps between the hopeful women in front of her, trying to get a glimpse into the house. Suddenly a man hollered, then she saw a hairy hand appear at the doorway. "All right. Let's begin!"

Shui-lian and Jin-lin followed the others through a narrow hallway and crowded into a room. A wooden desk and chair was the only furniture to speak of. Behind the desk sat a large man, drinking tea directly from the spout of a clay pot. A matchstick protruded from the corner of his mouth. One by one, he beckoned the women with a curled finger, and one by one he dismissed them with a backhand gesture, as if he were chasing away a fly.

"Listen, all of you," he shouted, the matchstick leaping up and down. "I came all the way here to look for young women workers, not to put together a regiment of old mothers and wives. You're wasting my precious time!"

Mean son of a bitch, Shui-lian cursed silently. When the man waved her forward, he looked her up and down several times, then smiled, the matchstick pointing skyward. To his questions Shui-lian lied that she was seventeen and that she was unattached—no thanks, she thought, to her mother's attempt to match her with the ugly boatman.

"Per—fect," he laughed, letting go of the matchstick. "Call me Da-Ge—Elder Brother—will you?"

"Sure, if that's what you wish. You're the boss," Shui-lian answered calmly, hiding her contempt for his stupid suggestion. Why don't you take a look at yourself in a mirror? she thought. You're old enough to be a father to most of us, including the wives and mothers you've sent away. But for once Shui-lian held her tongue. She remembered her mother's saying that when you live in someone else's house, you should bend your head if the ceiling is too low—a peculiar homily coming from someone who had never lived in a house. Shui-lian looked away, avoiding Da-Ge's appraising squint.

Da-Ge talked funny, with a strange accent that was hard to understand. He wasn't a local, that was for sure. Shui-lian supposed that was how people from big cities talked. She'd have to get used to it.

By the time the sun had climbed over to the other side of the roof, Shui-lian, Jin-lin, and three other young women had been sitting on the dirt floor in a backroom for hours, waiting for Da-Ge's final decision. There was barely any furniture in this room either, and the small, single window was too high for them to see outside. From the other room they heard only the murmurs of voices, the outer door opening and closing. Shui-lian tried to contain her edginess, wondering if her lie about her age would be found out. Her anxiety was so unsettling that she felt as if half a dozen buckets were moving up and down inside her chest.

All heads swung to the plank door when it was thrown open. All eyes focused on Elder Brother as he strutted into the room, followed by one of his helpers.

"I just finished talking to my boss on the phone," he said cheerfully, holding up a black object foreign to Shui-lian. "He wants me to return to Shanghai immediately because our recruiting quotas have been met ahead of schedule." Da-Ge paused for reaction, then continued. "It's a pity. I'd planned to stay in this region for a couple of days and hire at least a few dozen more young workers like you, but," he shrugged, "things've changed."

"What are you trying to say?" Shui-lian demanded, ignoring a nudge in her back. She was thirsty and hungry and tired of waiting. "Do you want us or not? Spit it out!"

"Aren't you a little red pepper!" Da-Ge laughed, throwing his head back. "Of course I want you, all five of you. And I hope you're grateful, because I'm the one who persuaded the big boss to take you." He waved his phone again to make his point. "But he wants us to leave for Shanghai right away, which means no time for you to go back and say farewell to your families."

"Not even a couple of hours?" one young woman asked in a quavering voice. "We can't just leave without saying goodbye."

Da-Ge ignored her and turned to look at Shui-lian and Jin-lin. "How about you two? Don't tell me you already miss your mommy and daddy. I've chosen you over the others because I thought you were different." He smirked.

"That suits me fine," Shui-lian spoke, fixing her eyes on Jin-lin, who seemed to hesitate.

"But we brought nothing with us for the trip, Da-Ge," Jin-lin pleaded, biting her lip. "No food, not even a change of clothes."

Elder Brother burst out laughing. "You're worried about your clothes? Listen to me, ladies. You're going to Shanghai, where every store is stuffed with beautiful clothes and shoes like you've never seen in your life. You'll find everything you'll ever need or want for your hair, skin, even your toenails!" He winked awkwardly. "Stop worrying! The sooner we hit the road, the earlier you'll get there and start work and make money to buy everything you've ever dreamed of. Believe me, in no time you will be as beautiful as movie stars."

He paused again, patting his chest. "Don't worry about a thing. Trust your Da-Ge to look after all your needs—your food, transportation, and lodging. After you arrive in Shanghai, you can eat anything you want. If you desire, you can have fish every day!"

He prattled on and on, drunk on his own words. What a blockhead, thought Shui-lian, shaking her head, bragging to a river *ku-li*'s daughter about eating fish.

The matter seemed settled, yet as soon as Da-Ge led them through the backroom and out of the house, two of the young women took off running, each in a different direction.

"Hey!" Da-Ge shouted, his face pale with anger. "Where are you going?"

The women quickly disappeared into the maze of laneways. Da-Ge turned to Shui-lian, Jin-lin, and the third young woman, who stood with her eyes fixed on her feet. "Are you going to run off like those ungrateful dogs?"

"I'm staying," Shui-lian said again.

Jin-lin sounded hesitant. "Me too."

The third woman, twisting the end of one of her pigtails around her finger, nodded.

Soon, an ancient-looking flatbed truck clattered to a halt before them. Elder Brother directed the three young women to climb into the back of the truck and sit on the mouldy straw, then hoisted himself into the cab. After a brief, bumpy ride, the truck stopped at a roadside restaurant. Throughout the meal—a bowl of rice noodles—Shui-lian kept her eyes diverted from Elder Brother and the driver and trained on her friend instead. Jin-lin looked like she was going to break into tears at any minute. Shui-lian fought off her own doubts and sadness, reminding herself that in order to have a better life she would have to *chi-ku*—eat bitterness—first. Later, in the back of the truck, leaning against the cab, half-listening to the yapping of Elder Brother and the driver, Shui-lian stretched her neck to look over the side of the vehicle and get a sense of where she was. Everything seemed strange, even the rivers and the mountains. That's because I've seen them only from the deck of a riverboat, she thought. Soon the towns and villages fell behind, and the mountains and clouds merged with the horizon. Later still, all was swallowed by darkness.

Shui-lian crossed her arms on top of her bended knees and lowered her head, wondering if her mother and brother were worried and looking for her. It then dawned on her that this would be her first night away from her family boat since she was born. She had cursed living on water for as long as she could remember, yet sitting in the dark on the rattling truck between

Jin-lin and the other young woman, she wished she could see the rivers one last time.

SHUI-LIAN AWOKE to the gabble of unknown voices. She raised her head, blinking and rubbing her eyes hard, and saw that a dozen more women had joined them in the back of the truck.

"We're near a train station," Jin-lin told her cheerfully, which brought a smile to Shui-lian's face. Shui-lian had never been on a train but had seen plenty of them zipping along the tracks beside the riverbanks. She let out a sigh of relief and closed her eyes again, hoping she'd be in Shanghai soon.

But before long Shui-lian began to feel as if she were caught in the guerrilla warfare she had read about at the floating school. She and the others got on the train all right, in the middle of the night, but hours later they were herded off like ducklings and into a minibus with blacked-out windows. A short ride later, they were hustled out of the bus and shoved into a shed with narrow cots lined up against windowless walls, then ordered to sleep.

Da-Ge travelled with them the entire time and seemed to know what he was doing, but he told no one where they were or what route they were taking, and snapped at anyone who dared to ask. Most of the time he let his first finger do the talking, pointing the young women out the shed door and onto a bus, or off the train and into a different vehicle. After two days the pattern became clear to Shui-lian. They would board the train late at night and get off before dawn broke, to be taken to a rundown house or shabby hut to rest until night fell again. There was no opportunity to wash, no soap, no running water. Then they were on the road again.

On the fourth night, after the young women were dropped off in front of a decrepit warehouse, Da-Ge announced that they would not be catching another train but were going to stay there for the entire night. Shui-lian welcomed the news like everyone else. By now she felt like a walking corpse, disoriented and exhausted, dirty and smelly and homesick. Jin-lin looked no better. As everyone rushed inside the building, Shui-lian lingered outside, wondering where they were. The night sky gave little light, but the monotonous drone of frogs told her a pond or a paddy field must be nearby. The solitude felt overwhelmingly odd for someone who had grown up in a province inhabited by more than a hundred million people.

Inside, a single light bulb burned weakly at the end of a wire, as if it, too, were suffering from fatigue. Unlike the other places they had stayed, this one had a cement rather than a dirt floor, cool and rough against Shui-lian's bare soles. Beds with rusty metal frames had been set up against one wall, each with a woven straw mat on wood planks, a pillow, and a thin blanket. Coloured plastic sheets hung between the beds—a pathetic attempt at privacy, thought Shui-lian bitterly, considering what they had been through the past four days.

"This looks like a workers' dorm!" one woman said cheerily. "We're close to Shanghai for sure!"

Her words were hailed by loud laughter and babbling. Two of the women started singing.

Da-Ge walked in and handed out small bars of soap and towels. "Good news," he crowed. "We'll be in Shanghai tomorrow. To celebrate, you'll have hot noodles to eat tonight, and fresh water for washing. So get yourself cleaned up and ready for the big city!"

Before the sound of his words hit the ground, everyone was chirping about their plans and their bright future. By the time the food arrived—bowls of thin noodle soup with pork fat and bits of cabbage floating on top—Shui-lian and Jin-lin had decided they would room together in Shanghai to save money.

"Who knows," Jin-lin chuckled, "maybe one day we can open our own business. It's allowed now, you know. The government even encourages it, praising anyone who makes money. If we work hard, maybe we'll both become boss women!"

Shui-lian smiled, feeling a buzz travelling through her nerves, anticipating the new life she had dreamed of for so long. It was all about to become real in a matter of hours, or, at most, days.

Shui-lian and Jin-lin chatted on amid the slurping of noodles. After they had washed and stretched out under the blankets—which smelled of sweat and mould—they whispered their hopes and dreams into the darkness. Behind the flimsy plastic partitions, they could hear other plans growing bigger and more extravagant, and the future burned brighter with every passing minute.

Chapter Five

Pan-pan

"Everything is set to go."

Dad's voice at the doorway brought Pan-pan back to the present. "Leave the porridge for now, Pan-pan. Come out and take a look."

Pan-pan shook her head to clear her thoughts. Quickly she dried her hands on her apron, took it off, and headed out of the kitchen. The image of the paper and bamboo house returned to her mind, along with the rigid, glass-eyed chickens. She wondered what other new and unexpected items awaited her.

The morning sun had risen over the first hill, and a rooster crowed in the distance. A couple more joined in half-heartedly. Nearby, her neighbour's dog barked. In the centre of the front yard, Mom's house now stood on the hard-packed earth, glowing in the pale sunlight. Before Pan-pan had a chance to look inside, a large black object protruding from the far side of the wobbling wall caught her eyes. Curious, she walked over to have a closer look.

"A paper car?" she burst out, frowning hard.

"Yes, a car!" her father, who had followed her over, responded cheerfully. "Wouldn't your mother be pleased?"

Pan-pan felt her breath blocked in her throat. Then her eyes fell on something inside the vehicle. A man carved from wood! He had on a real black jacket and hat. His white-gloved hands were wired to a plastic steering wheel. And he was grinning from ear to ear.

"A hired driver," her father gushed as if reading her mind. "What do you think?"

Pan-pan didn't know what to make of it all. On the one hand she marvelled at the skill of the craftspeople who had created the house, the furniture, the car—even the chickens; on the other hand, she found herself resenting such an extravagant way of worshipping the dead. She had heard that in the past the government banned the practice, condemning it as superstitious, even counter-revolutionary. But lately, although many old customs had been swept away by reforms and changes, many had returned. The business of venerating the deceased hadn't just made a comeback, it had become an industry. In her village, a silent war had broken out as neighbours competed to see who could come up with the most up-to-date items to offer to their relations who had left this world for the next. To save face, some families had gone deeply into debt. Each house had been larger and grander than the one before, filled with furniture and appliances, all made of colourful paper and sticks—objects that couldn't be found even in the households of the living. But in Yunxi Village nobody had ever produced a paper car and a wooden driver.

"Awesome, isn't it?"

Pan-pan turned to find Xin-Ma behind her, holding Gui-yang in her arms.

"It's okay, I guess."

"Just okay?" Dad said. "They did an excellent job. Don't you think so?"

From the corner of her eye, Pan-pan saw the eagerness on her father's face. "Yes, they surely did," she added. "But a driver? It's a little spooky, Dad."

"What's the good of having a car with no driver to take your mother around in the afterworld? In Guiyang all the important people and rich folks have drivers," Xin-Ma said in her husband's defence. "It cost your father a lot of money. Be grateful."

"I am."

"You don't look it."

"How am I supposed to look?" Pan-pan muttered. She had been feeling tense for the last few days, like everyone else in the house. Ah-Po had warned her again before turning off the light the night before, "Remember, don't let anything spoil the big day for your mother. The last thing your father needs is another row between you and Xin-Ma."

Wonderful or not, she thought with irritation, by the end of the day, house, chickens, car, and driver will be burned to ashes. Yes, it cost Dad a fortune, and yes, she should feel grateful. But still … "It's, it's … marvellous," she said, earning a smile from her father and Xin-Ma.

"NAN-MO-OMI-DA-FO. Nan-mo-omi-da-fo." The monks' monotonous chanting and praying, along with the clang of gongs and

thump of drums went on all morning, with breaks only for snacks, which the monks gobbled up as if noisemaking were hard labour. Leaning against the kitchen door frame, Pan-pan watched them for a while. All twelve, in their black robes with strips of black cloth tightly wrapped around their ankles and little caps, sat around the square dinner table. Mom's framed photograph had been placed in the centre, surrounded by burning red candles and smoking incense sticks projecting from bowls of sand. From time to time the monks rose sombrely, shuffled outside in single file, and tramped around Mom's house, droning their prayer songs. Little Gui-yang tottered after them, round and round, shrieking with delight.

Shortly after lunch, as Pan-pan returned home from her family's vegetable plot, a hoe over her shoulder and a basket of *qing-cai*—green cabbage—dangling from its end, she saw Gui-yang scampering toward her, his face bright with enthusiasm. The toddler lost his balance and fell headlong into the dirt. Pan-pan dropped her hoe, rushed over, and swept him up, cuddling him and cooing as she brushed soil from his button nose. Unconcerned, her half-brother giggled and strained to wriggle free, reaching toward the droning monks.

"Pan-pan! How many times do I have to tell you not to hold Gui-yang in your arms?" Xin-Ma appeared in front of her, a broom in her hand.

"I'm sorry. I forgot," Pan-pan said, feeling the familiar hot flush of irritation rise to her face. Turning to pick up her hoe and basket, she cursed behind her teeth, "Why can't I carry my own brother the way I want to?"

Half an hour later, when Pan-pan was hunkered down beside the family's well at the back of the house rinsing the vegetables she had picked so that Ah-Po could stir-fry them with shreds of pork for the monks' dinner, a shadow fell across the washbasin. Quietly Xin-Ma put a low stool on the ground and sat down next to Pan-pan.

"I'm sorry I yelled at you," she said, keeping her voice low.

"You're his mother. You make the rules," Pan-pan shot back, refusing to meet Xin-Ma's eyes. "But for once I'd like to know what your problem is! Why can't I hold my brother the way I want?"

"Lower your voice!" Xin-Ma hissed, taken aback by Pan-pan's uncharacteristic burst of anger. "I don't want your father or Ah-Po to hear us. I'll explain. But now isn't the time. I'll tell—"

"Now!" Pan-pan said it louder. "I won't wait." She looked up, staring at Xin-Ma. Her eyes shone with determination.

Xin-Ma lowered her head and heaved a monumental sigh. "All right. But you must promise me that you won't raise your voice again and won't get angry at me. Not today at least. And you must never let your father or Ah-Po know that I'm the one who told you this."

"Fine," Pan-pan answered grudgingly, shaking the water off the cabbage leaves before placing them in a basket. "I promise."

"The reason you can't carry Gui-yang in your arms is because … I'm sorry to say this … because you have very strong body odour. From your armpits. Where I come from, people call it 'fox stink.' Around here I don't know what it's—"

"I have what?" Pan-pan screeched and, despite herself, burst out laughing. "Are you telling me that my armpits smell like a fox? Is that another dumb story you've picked up from your rock-smashing co-workers?" she sneered.

Then she noticed the unusual expression on her stepmother's face. Sheepish. Almost guilty—and a look she had never seen Xin-Ma wear before. But most of all, it was Xin-Ma's silence in the face of Pan-pan's ridicule that spoke loud and clear. Pan-pan's attempt at humour gave way to a crushing humiliation, and she was swamped by a sense of shame as she realized that everybody except her must have known about her flaw.

"It's just an expression, as far as I know," Xin-Ma lamented, breaking the brief silence, stumbling over her words. "Some also call it dog or pig stink. I guess because those are the animals they're familiar with. I'm really sorry, Pan-pan. These are harsh words. And cruel. But you forced me to tell you."

"But I don't smell anything different about myself!" Pan-pan protested, a warm flush again rising to her face. Unconsciously, she clamped her arms against her ribcage. "Do you?"

"I'm afraid I do. Especially when you have your period."

Pan-pan jumped to her feet, knocking the basket over and scattering the cabbage on the ground. "I don't believe you. Everybody smells during the curse," she shouted, "including you!"

"Keep your voice down," Xin-Ma pleaded, looking up at Pan-pan, then in the direction of the house. "Listen to me. I'm not making this up. You're different. It's a very distinct odour. It's not an illness if that's what you're worried about. How can I put it?" She bit her lower lip, blinking her eyes rapidly. "It's … it's something you're born with. Some people believe it's also highly contagious, passed from person to person by touching, sharing clothes, even by mixing laundry."

Xin-Ma stumbled on, offering one explanation after another, but Pan-pan's mind had gone somewhere else. Suddenly certain events started to make sense, including changes that had occurred in the past year, particularly Ah-Po's odd behaviour, such as announcing one night shortly after Pan-pan started her period that Pan-pan should sleep on a cot by herself because she "wasn't a girl anymore," and constantly reminding Pan-pan that she must wash her clothes separately from everyone else's. "Don't ever soak your laundry with mine," Ah-Po had admonished without explanation, leaving Pan-pan frustrated and confused.

But nothing had puzzled Pan-pan more than the night she woke up to find Ah-Po standing at the end of her cot, sniffing Pan-pan's cotton-padded jacket. The old woman had held up the coat with her fingertips as fearfully as if a monster were hidden in the sleeves, ready to jump out and bite off her nose. A week later Ah-Po came home from the market with a strange present for Pan-pan: a tin filled with a sweet-smelling white powder. An image of a chubby baby's face was printed on the front, and the words *Heat Rash Powder* below it.

"What's this for?" Pan-pan had asked, giggling and turning the tin over in her hand, puzzled. "It's not even the rainy season yet. Besides, I'm a bit old for this, aren't I?"

"It's not just for infants," Ah-Po had replied defensively. "Anyone can use it. See?" She pulled open the lid. "It has such a nice smell. I heard that it's good for young skin." She then gave

Pan-pan detailed instructions on how to clean her armpits properly: wash at least once a day with soap and a good rinse, and then dust with lots of powder. The unwelcome tin had been sitting on the window sill above the stone sink ever since.

"Why didn't somebody tell me?" Pan-pan asked Xin-Ma. "All of you must have known that keeping this from me was like trying to hide fire inside a paper bag." Pan-pan felt another wave of humiliation in her stomach. "Is this why the girls in the village have been acting so strange toward me? And giving all kinds of stupid excuses to stay away from me? They all know, and they're all afraid that I'll pass it on to them!"

Pan-pan started to cry as the weight of realization further crushed her, her tears falling onto the front of her new jacket. "That's why I'm not allowed to hold your precious little boy! That's why I can only carry him piggyback." She managed a sneer as she mimicked Xin-Ma's accent.

Xin-Ma opened her mouth, but no words came out. She shook her head and looked away. Pan-pan too fell silent, until a thought crossed her mind. "Since fox stink is infectious, why did you say that I was born with it? Oh, I don't understand it at all! Why me? Why didn't somebody tell me?"

"Nobody, especially your Ah-Po, wanted to hurt your feelings. And your father—well, you know him. He doesn't like to face unpleasant things. We've all been afraid of your reaction. Especially after what happened to your mother—" Xin-Ma quickly clapped her hand over her mouth.

"My mother? What's all this got to do with her? Are you telling me Mom also had fox stink?"

A loud shout interrupted Pan-pan's flood of questions. Her father poked his head out of the back door. "Hey, you two! It's time!"

"Listen, Pan-pan," Xin-Ma whispered worriedly, hastily gathering up the vegetables. "I'm already in deep trouble for telling you this. Go now. The final ceremony is about to begin. I beg you, save your questions for tomorrow."

Inside the house, a small, square mat had been laid on the floor in front of the table where the monks had been sitting and praying for hours. Bowls of freshly cooked meat and vegetables, steamed rice, roasted peanuts, and sunflower seeds were arranged before the photograph of Pan-pan's mother. Her smiling eyes seemed to set on Pan-pan the moment Pan-pan stepped into the room and to follow her every movement. Standing, the monks took up their chant again. When her name was called by the head monk, Pan-pan walked up to the edge of the rug and got down on her knees the way her father had done a moment before.

"One *ke-tou,*" the monk intoned. Pan-pan placed one hand on each side of the mat and lowered her forehead until it touched the cold concrete floor. Following the commands of "two *ke-tou,* three *ke-tou,*" Pan-pan repeated the action as she struggled to hold back her tears, overwhelmed by the ache that her mother's absence always brought to her heart. The head monk had warned her earlier that tears would chase away the soul of the deceased, which was present during the ceremony. Mom, Pan-pan wept inside, why didn't you tell me that I had a terrible smell? Was that what you meant by calling me your imperfect child?

Chapter Six

Shui-lian

Shui-lian rose slowly from the depths of a dream in which she lay in the bottom of a boat rocked by choppy waves. As consciousness returned, she remembered where she was—in a warehouse with other hopeful young women, on the last stage of a long journey. Soon she would be in Shanghai, a factory worker. She smiled to herself in the darkness.

Then she became aware of a weight pressing on her bed. Rough fingers crawled at the waistband of her underpants. The elastic gave way with a rip, and her eyes snapped open. Terror struck her, driving the air from her lungs. A shadow loomed over her. The stink of rice wine and garlic in her face was as real as the sharp stubble that scraped her cheek as a man lowered himself onto her, grunting and grinding his body against hers. Shui-lian struggled, pushed against him, and yelled for help, only to realize that from behind the partitions similar shrieks were ringing out. She twisted her torso under the man's weight and tried to free herself by raising her knees, but he was too heavy. Cursing, stricken with panic, Shui-lian pounded the attacker's back with her fists as she flung her head from side to side. In desperation, she raked his face with her nails.

"Get off me, you filthy son of a dog!" she screamed, digging her nails in deeper.

"Ow! You bitch!" the man howled. He swung his head aside to avoid her fingers, then smashed his fist into Shui-lian's face. Clutching a handful of Shui-lian's hair, he slammed her head against the thin mat. Sparks flew before her eyes. The ache in her skull was unbearable.

Then Shui-lian felt something near her groin. She cried out in pain as the man jammed himself into her. She gasped for air but couldn't breathe. Wailing and pleading tore the air around her, reminding Shui-lian that this was no nightmare.

At length, the man got off her, huffing heavily in the darkness. Groaning, Shui-lian curled up and rolled onto her side. It's finally over, she said to herself. It's finished. But, a few seconds later, she heard a low laugh and the shuffle of feet, before someone else grabbed her and turned her onto her back. A second assault began. Clenching her teeth and squeezing her eyes shut, Shui-lian repeated to herself, Let it be finished or let me be finished.

By the time the intruders had stolen away, Shui-lian was barely conscious, despite the groaning and weeping nearby her and the sea of revolting smells—sweat, vomit, and blood. One by one, shadows emerged from behind the curtains and made their way to the sinks. Standing on wobbly legs, turning the tap with a shaking hand, Shui-lian tried to comprehend what had happened. Behind her, others moved around like ghosts, avoiding each other's eyes.

Shui-lian scrubbed raw every inch of her exposed flesh and used up the small bar of soap washing and rewashing her face and thighs. Her guts on fire, her head aching, she was not sure if she would ever clean the men's stink from her skin and the shame from her body. Bruised and disoriented, she pulled on her clothes, ripped the soiled blanket and straw mat off the bed, and lay down on the bare planks.

"Ruined," she heard Jin-lin crying on the next bed. "Now no man will want me for a wife. I'll never have the face to go back to see my family again!"

Still in shock, Shui-lian didn't reply, but anger was slowly building up inside her the way the rivers of Sichuan swelled after a violent storm. She lay curled into a ball, hugging herself, staring dry eyed at nothing until pale light seeped under the door.

Before noon there was a knock on the door. Shui-lian lifted her head and saw Da-Ge sidle into the room like a crab. Most of the women averted their eyes. Looking sorrowful and choking as though heartbroken, Da-Ge told them that he'd been badly beaten by the intruders, thrown hard to the ground, then tied hand and foot. He was lucky to be alive, he said mournfully, letting out a few dry coughs to show his suffering and pain.

Shui-lian fixed him with a hateful look. For a man who claimed to have been attacked and trussed up, he had no welts on his wrists and his pie-shaped face was free of cuts and bruises.

Thumping his chest with his open palm, Da-Ge vowed that if the young women kept what had happened to themselves, he wouldn't tell a living soul either. "Don't worry, I'll keep your secret. It's over now. Let's put this behind us and look forward to the future," he soothed, parroting an insincere government slogan. "In life, we have to make small sacrifices in order to score big gains," he added, turning and pretending to limp out the door.

"*We?* Small sacrifice?" Shui-lian spat, pulling down the torn plastic partition. "That son of a turtle makes it sound as though this is what we should have expected. We have to do something about it." Her remark was confronted with silence.

Half an hour later, the minibus with the blacked-out windows picked them up. After a short ride, during which every one of them tried in vain to find a comfortable sitting position, the bus pulled to a halt in front of a small, dilapidated roadside inn. Shui-lian and Jin-lin were lodged in a tiny room with a smooth dirt floor. But at least there was a toilet and a sink with running water—heavenly luxuries which failed to lift their spirits.

Da-Ge had given each of them a cloth-wrapped parcel containing a pair of sandals, a couple of shirts, pants, and socks. Some of the clothing was new and some used, but it was all clean—a great improvement over the rags they'd been wearing for days.

"Tomorrow will be your big day," he had declared with false cheer after passing out the packages. "Your new boss is coming to get you. Make yourselves presentable."

"How are we supposed to do that?" Jin-lin had wheezed, her left eye purple and swollen, the rip at the corner of her mouth still leaking blood each time she opened her mouth. "We can barely walk!"

"That stinking bastard," Shui-lian hissed later that night as she lay beside Jin-lin on the wide platform bed. "I'd like to strangle him, or hold his head under water and watch him drown. Does he really think we fell for that pathetic story of his? All this happened because of him! Either he planned it or he let it happen."

"But what can we do?" Jin-lin said. "We're under his power until our new boss comes to collect us. We don't even know where we are."

"We're in hell," said Shui-lian, pounding her fist against the thin mattress. "I wonder if the factory will still take us, seeing us in such a state."

For the first time since they had known each other, Jin-lin had no answer.

Even though they were both exhausted, they were unable to sleep, starting at every creak or rustle outside the window, each footfall that floated into their room from the corridors. Shui-lian stayed awake most of the night. The slightest sound made her jump and shake with fear.

The next morning, Shui-lian and Jin-lin filed into the canteen with the others and sat down to a bowl of rice gruel and pickled vegetables. Shui-lian had to force the food down, for she had no appetite. As she scooped gruel into her mouth, she heard the screech of brakes outside, a muffled shout, and then the tramp of feet on the path. The door flew open and a tall man strode into the room, followed by three more men, who immediately fanned out to block the exits. They all wore the uniforms of the Public Security Bureau.

"Police!" Jin-lin hissed, her eyes wide.

"All of you! You are under arrest!" The leader bawled. "For prostitution."

Chapter Seven

Pan-pan

Pan-pan felt like she was in a heavy fog the rest of the day, speaking to no one unless spoken to. As the afternoon dragged on, with the continuous racket of drums and gongs, she couldn't wait for the monks to leave.

Finally, as the sun shifted farther westward and sank behind the mountains, everyone in the village, it seemed, gathered in front of Pan-pan's home and watched her father slowly and with great formality approach the house of gold paper. Solemnly he kneeled, struck a match, touched it to the corner of the front wall, and then tossed it into the paper automobile. In less than a minute the structure was engulfed in flames. The paper curled and sparkled; the bamboo sticks crackled fiercely. A huge ball of fire lifted off the ground and rose, nearly reaching the electric wires overhead. Heat and black smoke drove the onlookers back. The model furniture and appliances, as well as the chickens, the car, and the driver—all were swallowed by the hungry flames within minutes. Glowing ashes danced and swirled in the air before falling to the ground. Mom's house was on its way to the afterworld. Pan-pan's eyes trailed after a large piece of ash slowly drifting toward the fields, wishing, through her tears and the deep sobs that shook her to the core, that her mother's spirit would stay.

"LET'S FACE IT, my child, I'm a farmer—or I used to be," began Pan-pan's father, a bitter smile on his bony face. "We're peasants. Who in the world knows more about smells and odours, stinks and fragrances? We live with them day after day, year after year. We sense them all, and we don't give a damn!"

It was the morning after the ceremonial offering and fire, and her father had sat Pan-pan down at the table. Her mother's photo still stood in the centre. Ah-Po had made herself scarce, remaining in her room, and Xin-Ma, her puffy eyes telling that she too had passed a sleepless night, had taken Gui-yang out for a walk.

Pan-pan's father's face was pale and drained, the same colour as the ashes scattered across the yard, as though the fire had also extinguished something inside him.

"When your mother was a girl, she wasn't bothered by her strong body odour until your aunt Cai-fei put a name to it and told her it was a condition only a few suffered from. I blame Cai-fei to this day. As far as I understand, it's the work of a person's sweat glands. Some people perspire more than others, so it's only normal they smell stronger. But 'fox stink'?" He swallowed hard, shaking his head. "What kind of ignorance is that? For one thing, I've never seen a fox in my life, let alone smelled one. I would never have wasted my time listening to such rubbish if it hadn't been your mom telling me this."

He soon forgot about the whole thing, her father continued, because at that time, in the eyes of the government and the Party ideology, emphasizing personal needs, even hygiene and appearance, was condemned as unrevolutionary. Bourgeois vanity, it was called. The more you gave in to your individual concerns, the less you were committed to the Communist cause. In those days, the villagers competed to see who could appear the dirtiest and smell the worst, so they would be praised as pure proletarians. "As a matter of fact, your mother was often the target of such criticism simply because cleanliness and femininity were important to her. Once, she was accused of smelling like a flower because growing flowers and even houseplants was denounced as self-indulgent."

Pan-pan's father sipped his green tea and shook his head again. Then came the changes and reforms, he explained, which brought new ways of living and thinking. Everything was turned upside down. Wrong didn't just become right, it was sought after. Even the fashion industry, which had been banned for decades as rotten capitalist rubbish, returned with a vengeance and made its way even to backwater places such as Tongren. During her visit to Yunxi Village at Lunar New Year, Cai-fei showed Pan-pan's mother a poster she had peeled off an electric pole on Tongren's main street. The flyer advertised a special treatment that cured fox stink. Easy and fast, it said. In and out the same day. Guaranteed results.

"That damn flyer stirred up the whole thing again, like blowing on dying embers," her father continued angrily. "I wasn't totally surprised that such nonsense would gain ground since everything modern or stylish that could make money was called a new trend. Everybody, it seemed, was chasing after money. But I didn't expect your mom would buy into this and go to such an extreme. It was around the time when the whole country was worried about some kind of bug that would eat up words and numbers stored in computers when the new millennium arrived, like rice borers devouring our crops.

"After the New Year celebration, Cai-fei returned home but left the flyer with us. She had raised your mother's hopes that she could get rid of her social handicap once and for all—and that's what she called it, a social handicap. I had no idea she'd been feeling that way, and for so long. I tried to talk her out of it but failed miserably. She wouldn't even let me go with her to Tongren for the operation, saying it was only day surgery and that she would be home in no time."

Pan-pan's father told of how Cai-fei took Pan-pan's mother to a two-room flat on the second floor of an apartment building in downtown Tongren. There was no sign on the door, just the unit number. The young woman in a white gown who let them in asked for payment before they even sat down. The doctor, also in a white robe and cap, greeted them with a heavy accent Cai-fei said was not local. He insisted that Cai-fei not come into the operating room because it was sterile—that seemed like a sign of high standards. Cai-fei watched as her sister was led away, confident that things looked official and promising.

"Then through the thin wall she told me she could hear the snips of scissors and the groans of your mother," Pan-pan's father went on. "It's surgery, she reminded herself. It's only natural to suffer some pain and discomfort."

Cai-fei brought her sister home to recuperate. One day passed, then two, but the swelling wouldn't go down. If anything, it grew worse. Pan-pan's mother couldn't move her arms, and the angry red welts in her armpits festered. Each time Cai-fei went back to the doctor, he assured her that everything was normal, swelling was to be expected and so was the pain, and sent her away with stronger painkillers.

"But your mother must have sensed that something had gone terribly wrong," said Pan-pan's father, his voice quaking. "By the end of the week, she asked Cai-fei to bring her home. And you know the rest of it."

Yes, I do, thought Pan-pan bitterly, recalling the day Mom was carried into the house on a stretcher, pale and motionless, a heavy quilt pulled up to her chin. It was clearly a strain for her even to greet Pan-pan and offer a weak smile.

"But I still don't understand what she died from."

"From infection," Xin-Ma cut in. She had come into the room and taken a seat beside her husband. "The doctor botched the operation. After your mother's funeral, your father went to Tongren to confront the doctor, but instead of a clinic he found an empty apartment. No one in the building was able to tell him who the doctor was or where he'd gone. The building supervisor was shocked to learn the flat had been used for surgery. Your father searched the city for the man, wandering the streets for days. All he got for his trouble was a bagful of advertisements he ripped off electric poles and walls, offering surgery to enlarge breasts or eyes, shrink and reshape noses, and to cure fox stink and other body odours."

"What a waste, Pan-pan," Dad repeated, drying his eyes on his sleeve. "Your mother died for nothing!"

"But why didn't she tell me about all that?"

"Shame, I guess," her father murmured. "Shame for her condition. Shame for the way she was regarded by some villagers. And she was scared for you, afraid you might have inherited the same thing. She said to me the night before she left for Tongren that if she had the operation and it worked, then she'd know where to take you if you wanted to get it done."

FOR THE NEXT THREE DAYS, Pan-pan mostly kept to herself, thinking and sorting things out inside her head. More than once her eyes rose to the tops of the purple mountains and she felt the familiar tug of new and strange places behind the peaks and beyond. On the fourth day, she was waiting for her father when he returned from a long walk around the village. He had decided to delay his return to the construction site because of what had happened at home. Pan-pan watched him hang up his jacket and change his shoes before joining the family at the supper table. As soon as he was settled, Pan-pan took a deep breath and began to speak.

"Dad, Ah-Po, and Xin-Ma, I've got something to tell you." She stopped, casting a nervous glance around her. "I've decided to leave home to find a job. I want to go to Beijing."

Silence fell. All three adults stared at her, then at one another, as though a stranger had wandered in from the fields and taken Pan-pan's place.

"No, you can't! I won't let you!" Ah-Po spoke first, jabbing her chopsticks in the air to make her point.

"Ridiculous," Xin-Ma grumbled, frowning. "You're still a kid."

Pan-pan's father slowly put down his chopsticks and stared at the bowl of rice in front of him, giving Pan-pan an uneasy feeling. She'd have preferred to hear him say something, even shout at her—anything but the pained look in his eyes.

"Hear me out, Dad," she said. "My decision has very little to do with what I've learned about Mom or me. The truth is, I've been thinking about leaving for some time—from the day you went away to look for work in the cities. So many people in the village have done the same thing. There's a whole world out there that I know nothing about."

"But why Beijing? Why so far away?" Xin-Ma interrupted.

"Because it's the capital," Pan-pan answered right away. "Ever since I was a child and listened to Ah-Po talking about the girl from Beijing I've dreamed of seeing the famous sights with my own eyes. Now that it's allowed, I can live and look for a job there. If it doesn't work out, I can always come back." She paused and quickly looked around the table. "But first I plan to visit Auntie Cai-fei and go to the places Mom walked for the last time."

Gui-yang chose that moment to wake up. His cries carried easily from the backroom and Xin-Ma got up to go to him. As if he too had just awakened, Pan-pan's father began to rub the side of his face with one hand, back and forth over his stubbled chin, his eyes avoiding Pan-pan's.

It was Ah-Po who broke the tension. "If that's what you really want to do, I for one won't try to stop you." She swallowed hard and continued. "When the girl from Beijing was sent to the village to live with us she was about your age, so it's not the first time I've seen kids travel from place to place on their own. In those days, youngsters were forced to leave their homes in the city and come down to the countryside, to be re-educated by us peasants. I didn't understand it at all then, and I still don't. Why would the government send us more mouths to eat from our bowl of rice, which was only half full as it was?

"It was the government's doing at the time. Now it seems the same thing is happening again, only in reverse." Ah-Po stopped to catch her breath. "I try not to be too upset when I see skilled farmers like your father abandoning the fields, their homes, and their families to travel hundreds of kilometres to work in the cities. My head spins whenever I think about it. Look around here. Spring planting is coming up soon, but the fields lie unplowed. What's left behind in this village is an army of mothers and grandmothers and children. Maybe Beijing is not a bad choice, Pan-pan, since I have a connection there. The girl named Sun Ming. Remember, son?"

Dad lifted his eyes. "Yes. Sun Ming. I remember. It was a long time ago, though. I was only eight."

Ah-Po left the table and went to the room she and Pan-pan shared. Pan-pan could hear drawers open and shut. When she returned, Ah-Po sat down and unfolded a piece of lined paper on the tabletop. "Nearly thirty years," she murmured to herself as she slid the flattened paper across to Pan-pan. "This is her address. I wonder if she still lives there."

Chapter Eight

Shui-lian

As if the assaulted women at the inn had not suffered enough, the Public Security Bureau had charged every one of them with prostitution. Hysterical crying and panicked explanations echoed throughout the canteen amid the police sergeant's booming but useless orders to be quiet.

"We're not prostitutes!" Jin-lin pleaded over and over to one of the policemen, her voice trembling. "How could you even say such a thing?"

"We're on our way to work in Shanghai," Shui-lian told the stern-faced sergeant. "We were attacked in the middle of the night. If you don't believe me, go ask Da-Ge. He will tell you we're not lying."

A hoot of laughter burst out among the policemen. "Shanghai?" snarled one. "It's a blessing you don't look as stupid as you sound. You're in Anhui Province now, a long way north of Shanghai, and women like you are not welcome here."

"I don't believe you," Shui-lian shot back. "People's Policemen shouldn't tell lies. We've been recruited for factory work. In Shanghai," she repeated.

"Listen," a different cop put in. "You've been lied to, not by us, but by your so-called Da-Ge. And he's nowhere to be found." Shaking his head, he went on, his voice softer. "And there are no jobs waiting for you in Shanghai either. Trust me. Or half the population of this province would have left long ago."

Tears streamed down Shui-lian's face, and she let them run freely as she recalled the past five days. She knew there was no sympathy for a rape victim no matter how savagely she had been assaulted. Only rejection. Now they were openly condemned by the police.

Around her the desperate young women cried, leaning on one another's shoulders. Shui-lian turned to face the wall, dropped to her knees, and, wrapping her arms around herself, pressed her chin to her chest as if to prevent her dignity from slipping away. Surrounded by the dreadful wailing, she dried her eyes with her shirt sleeve, vowing that from now on she would shed no more tears in front of strangers.

LATER THAT DAY a middle-aged woman walked into the inn's canteen, where one remaining policeman had been keeping Shui-lian and the others under guard. The woman introduced herself as Comrade Guo, from the local branch of the Women's Federation of China, and the first thing she said was that the police had dropped the prostitution charge. She had a kindly face and gentle voice, but Shui-lian held back her trust. They should be thankful to the police force, Guo explained, otherwise by now they would all be scattered around over the region in individual households.

"This Da-Ge of yours had no intention of taking you to factories in Shanghai," she went on. "His plan all along was to force you into marriage."

"Marriage?" Jin-lin broke in, her voice shaking, her mouth hanging open. "Are you saying we would be married off to total strangers?"

"That's exactly what I'm telling you. And the grooms are more than just strangers. Most are in poor health or physically disabled, some even mentally ill. Men the local young women want to have nothing to do with."

"That pig!" Shui-lian cursed loudly, her eyes boring into Guo's.

Comrade Guo shook her head and continued. "I've no doubt that Da-Ge belongs to one of the gangs that abduct young women like you in poorer regions of the country, or in your case, trick them with stories of better lives and attractive job offers. He then sells them as wives to families in economically better areas that are hundreds, even thousands, of kilometres away from their homes. These new wives are trapped, their fate sealed, for they have no money, no way to get back home. If they escape they're hunted down and beaten and locked up. Businesses like his flourish because nowadays young women are in short supply in most parts of the country, especially in the countryside."

"How can that be?" Shui-lian asked. She didn't add that her own mother and brother had so eagerly tried to palm her off on an ugly boatman.

"Because the government decided to redistribute farmland to individual households and at the same time eased travel restrictions, allowing farmers to move from the countryside to cities to look for jobs," Guo replied. "As a result, lots of young women travel to the cities to avoid farm work, taking jobs as maids and nannies, even street sweepers and cleaners—practically any kind of work that the city folks look down upon. A few lucky ones find husbands there and become urban dwellers. Those who end up returning home have become pickier about their prospective husbands. On top of that, for over twenty years the birth rate of baby girls in the rural regions has been declining. Now there's a shortage of eligible wives. It's a crisis. That's what brought Da-Ge and gangsters like him into their dirty business."

"Are you saying we've been sold without our knowing it?" another young woman asked.

"Yes. Very likely the families have already paid him, and he and his helpers have run off with their money. They probably bought the clothes you're wearing."

"But why us?" Shui-lian murmured.

"Because you're poor, of course, and easily exploited. But I'm sure things will get better where you came from. Remember, when the river rises, so do the boats," Comrade Guo said quietly, quoting an expression Shui-lian had learned in school. "Girls, go back home. There is nothing for you here, believe me. If you can't afford the journey, the federation will buy tickets for you."

JIN-LIN AND SHUI-LIAN talked throughout the night, sorrow mixed with regret and despair. By the time the sky turned milky grey, their tears had run dry.

"This is all my fault," Jin-lin sobbed.

"Don't talk like that," said Shui-lian. "You didn't tie me up and drag me along with you. I'm responsible for myself!" Lowering her head, staring at her bare feet, Shui-lian thought for a minute before looking up again. "What are you going to do?"

"I'm going back home," Jin-lin replied. "I've had enough of this. I miss my family."

"But what about your father? He'll keep pestering you."

A scornful smile crossed Jin-lin's face. "Don't worry. I know how to handle him now. No one is ever going to hurt me that way again." She pressed her lips together. "How about you? You're coming with me, aren't you?"

"No, I don't want to go home," Shui-lian answered firmly. "I won't let that scum Da-Ge, or those raping bastards, ruin my plans. And I won't let my mother and brother force me to get married. That's no better than being raped, is it?"

Fighting off sympathy for the disappointment written on Jin-lin's face, Shui-lian explained that she had made up her mind even before Comrade Guo had finished talking. "Going back home would be like a fish swimming back to her little pond after seeing the big ocean. I still want to go to Shanghai," she concluded.

Hours later, outside the entrance to the inn, Shui-lian said goodbye to the other young women, who, like Jin-lin, had all decided to go home. Then the two friends stood together for a few awkward moments.

"I promise I'll look for your family's boat and go to see your mother as soon as I get back to Sichuan," Jin-lin said repeatedly, wiping her tears.

"Tell her not to worry. I'll be all right," Shui-lian replied, hoping she sounded more confident than she felt. She took Jin-lin in her arms and hugged her as hard as she could. Then she turned and started walking, her eyes straight ahead, leaving her childhood friend behind.

At a crossroads Shui-lian approached an old man who was roasting sweet potatoes on a coal stove.

"Which way to Shanghai?" she asked.

"East," the old man answered, pointing his blackened finger at the rising sun.

Chapter Nine

Pan-pan

The sun was sinking in the western sky when the train slowed down to enter Bengbu Station, the last major stop in Anhui Province. Pan-pan shifted her swollen feet, wriggling her toes to get rid of the numbness, only to see the last strand of her shoelace let go with a snap. Over three days now, ever since she boarded the train in Guiyang, she had watched her frayed shoelaces break off one loop after another, as if they were programmed on a timer. She had insisted on buying a ticket for the "slow train" to Beijing because it was cheapest. Her father, who had come to Guiyang to see her off, had wanted her to take the express. But no one had told her that "slow" meant the train stopped at practically every house that stood along the railway track. A donkey cart could have covered the same distance just as quickly, she grumbled to herself. She had a seat all right, one-third of a wooden bench with a hard back beside the window, yet it was far from relaxing and restful.

Her father had cautioned her time and again that she should apply double vigilance when the train stopped at a station. "Don't let your bag and bedroll out of your sight," he called out one last time as the train pulled away from the platform.

Although her belongings were now stowed securely on the luggage rack over her head, Pan-pan raised her eyes at each stop and stared at them until the train began moving again. She wondered if, by the time she reached the capital, she would become cross-eyed. You can never be too careful, Ah-Po's caution rang in her ears. She smiled inwardly each time she caught sight of her luggage. Never in her life had she had so many new things—clothes and shoes and socks, not to mention a brand-new quilt, a gift from Xin-Ma's hope chest. When the villagers heard about Pan-pan's journey, they had given her plenty of advice. Yet the only thing they had agreed on was that winter in the nation's capital was frigid. "It's a land of ice and snow, and knife-sharp winds," they warned her. "Watch out for your ears and nose or they'll freeze and fall off."

In Tongren, Auntie Cai-fei had reluctantly taken Pan-pan shopping, jamming a large vinyl bag full with a new cotton-padded jacket, pants, and shoes, a set of towels, and half a dozen washcloths, as well as two tiny bottles of scented water. All the while, as they went from one store to another, she uttered a stream of words to try to persuade Pan-pan to stay with her.

"You can find a job here. Tongren is not as grand as the capital, but it's not a village, either. You're only fifteen. Your mother would never let you go to Beijing if she were still alive."

Ah-Po's going-away package had been different and unexpected. The night before Pan-pan left for Tongren, she gave Pan-pan a shoulder bag made of faded green canvas with a red star stitched on the flap, like the ones soldiers used to carry. She told Pan-pan it had been left behind by Sun Ming, the Beijing girl.

Ah-Po had washed it and put it away with the piece of paper, and had forgotten about them both over the years.

"If you find her, I wonder if she'll recognize her bag," Ah-Po murmured as she laid it on the table, her wrinkled hand brushing the creased star. It was only after everyone else had gone to bed that Ah-Po presented Pan-pan with four hundred yuan folded neatly inside a handkerchief. It was the first time Pan-pan had seen so much money. She shook her head and pushed Ah-Po's hands away.

"No, Ah-Po, I can't," she said over and over again. "The money is for your *hou-shi*—your funeral arrangement."

"You silly girl, I'm still healthy and strong and can start saving again. Besides, if you find Sun Ming and a job in Beijing, you'll take care of things for me after I am gone from this world. If it makes you feel better, consider it a loan," she had said lightheartedly but with a forced smile. Later, she carefully sewed a pocket in Pan-pan's undershirt to keep the money in and secured it with a safety pin. "Don't spend it until you have to," she admonished. The lump had pressed against Pan-pan's chest ever since she left Guiyang.

And it turned out to be a long journey. Over the past few days Pan-pan had grown fed up with the click-clack of the steel wheels, the sway of the car, the constant nattering of strangers' conversations, and, most of all, the irritating cigarette smoke. It was Sun Ming's thirty-year-old address that kept her spirits up. She knew nothing about city living, but one look at Sun Ming's address was enough to fill her with excitement and anticipation. It had three sets of numbers and a dozen words! In Pan-pan's village there was no need for any kind of identification beyond the name of the recipient. Everyone knew where everyone else lived.

With one last lunge, the train came to a complete stop. Pan-pan let out a long sigh of relief. Only twelve hours more and her voyage would be over at last. She yawned, stretching her arms upward, her fingertips touching the cold wooden railing of the luggage rack.

"What's that awful smell!" the elderly woman next to Pan-pan burst out. Sniffing hard and blowing through her nostrils, she searched in both directions.

Pan-pan moaned quietly as a hot flush climbed up her neck and onto her face. Clutching her arms against her rib cage she turned her head away from the accusing looks of her neighbour, only to be caught by the intense, fearful stare of her own eyes reflected in the window. How could you be so careless and forgetful? she cursed herself. It ought to be etched in her mind by now. Suddenly she felt hungry and tired, crushed by the homesickness she had tried so hard to suppress since leaving her village. Her happiness at the prospect of an end to her journey, which had warmed her just a moment ago, vanished like thin smoke, replaced by a surge of anxiety that when the train reached its final destination, she would be left in a strange city totally alone. And by then she would be even farther away from home and the mountains in Guizhou.

"Deal with it when the time comes." Xin-Ma's motto sounded in her ears and calmed her a bit. Pan-pan stuck her head out the window, immersing herself in a sea of singsong vendors' voices. Some of the sellers ran alongside the train. Others stood next to carts piled high with cigarettes, drinks, fruit, and buns. Each tried to top the other, to attract buyers.

"Get your hot 'dog-won't-leave-them-alone' meat buns," an old man bellowed, pushing a three-wheel barrow. Wisps of steam rose from the tiers of a bamboo steamer.

"World-famous roasted Shandong peanuts," shouted another, a long pole balanced on his shoulder, a basket dangling from each end.

"Come, try some Anhui dates. The best and the sweetest under heaven."

Pan-pan swallowed hard as she watched the array of exotic foods paraded before her. The sounds and the aromas made her mouth water. For three days now she had eaten nothing but homemade flatbread, washed down with hot water provided on the train. Station after station, she had overcome the temptation to treat herself to the seemingly endless supplies of candies, nuts, cookies, sweet buns, and eggs boiled in tea and spices. Her money had to be put to better use, she kept reminding herself.

Another voice drifted by. "Delicious sunflower seeds roasted in five spices."

Pan-pan craned her neck farther, searching the crowd on the platform. Roasted sunflower seeds were her favourite snack, crispy and salty. And they shouldn't cost much since sunflowers were easy to grow—every household in the village planted them alongside the pathways, at the corners of buildings, and around ditches and ponds. The villagers roasted the seeds in woks with salt and then sprinkled them with sugar water, leaving a sweet and salty coating on the shells. But never had

Pan-pan heard of sunflower seeds roasted in five spices. They must taste even more delicious.

"Do I have time to get off the train to buy something?" Pan-pan asked the young woman who sat across from her.

"Sure. The train will be here for another twenty minutes. You'll have plenty of time."

Pan-pan hesitated, then pointed at the luggage rack above her head. "Will you look after my bag and bedroll?"

"Oh, come on, you peasant! Lighten up, will you? Who would steal a bedroll nowadays?" a woman across the aisle grumbled. She had tried a few times to change seats with Pan-pan so that she could sit beside the window, but Pan-pan had refused.

Pan-pan ignored her comment, though she'd noticed that lately almost no one coming onboard had bedrolls with them. And the bags they carried were much fancier than hers. Some even had wheels at the bottom, and the owners pulled them along effortlessly.

"Don't worry, I'll keep an eye on your things," the young woman assured her with a smile.

Picking up her small shoulder bag, Pan-pan dashed along the aisle and jumped down onto the platform. She zigzagged through the crowd, chasing after the sunflower-seed seller.

"I'll take one bag of your five-spices seeds, Uncle," she said, catching her breath.

The shabbily dressed man gave her a packet and held out his hand. "One yuan."

It was only then that Pan-pan remembered that all her money was in the pocket sewn into her shirt. She hesitated, looking at the triangular paper packet resting in her hand. Slowly she pushed her free hand up inside her jacket, her back arched into a bow as she reached for the money pouch. Turning aside to avoid the probing eyes of the seller, she opened the pouch and gingerly peeled off a five-yuan note, handing it to him.

Just then, something heavy struck her shoulder and a figure in a black coat flew by her, snatching the pouch from her hand. Pan-pan let out a loud cry. The paper parcel hit the ground and the roasted seeds scattered over the pavement.

"Thief! Help! Please help me!" Pan-pan shrieked as she sprinted after the fleeing woman. One of her laceless shoes flew off, then the other, but she kept running. Around the corner she skidded and fell headfirst on the ground. Scrambling to her feet, spitting blood, she dashed down the stairs and out onto the open tracks. The woman, her open jacket flapping as she ran, was too fast for Pan-pan. The rough gravel between the ties quickly tore her new socks to strips, jabbing her bare soles and bruising her ankles. But she continued the chase, crying and yelling for help as she ran. Through tear-filled eyes, she saw the thief turn and run behind a house on the road ahead, out of sight. Pursuing the woman, Pan-pan found herself at a busy intersection. She stopped, panting. Frantically, she looked to her left and her right, up the street and down the other way, hoping the thief would reappear. There was no one, only the traffic. The thief was gone. Pan-pan wailed in frustration. Suddenly, all the moving objects—the horse carts, tractors, cars, and trucks—seemed to be charging toward her. With a moan, she passed out, collapsing onto the sidewalk.

蓮水相逢

Part Two

Lian shui xiang feng

Lotus and water depend on each other.

Chapter Ten

When Pan-pan came to, she found herself stretched out on a wooden bench. Slowly she sat up, rubbing her eyes. Her head ached. She touched a sore spot on her forehead and winced. Licking her dry, swollen lips, she tasted blood. Her feet were bare and sore; they felt to Pan-pan like they had been pounded with a hammer.

Confused, Pan-pan looked around, scanning the faces of people seated on the benches across from her. The place was too noisy to be a hospital. It was only when her wandering eyes noticed piles of luggage between the aisles that she realized she was in the waiting room of a railway station.

Hobbling to the window, she stared out at the empty tracks. There was no train. She looked about her but didn't see her bag and bedroll. When she reached for her money pouch, she remembered what had happened. Pan-pan groaned in despair and sank back onto the bench. Everything—her money, her bedroll and bag—were gone. Even the train had left without her. She covered her face with her hands and sobbed.

Footsteps approached and stopped. A tall middle-aged man wearing a railway uniform and cap stood before her, holding her shoes. He sat down and introduced himself. Lao Ma told Pan-pan in a hushed voice that a horse-cart driver had discovered her lying on the sidewalk and brought her back to the train station after finding a cancelled train ticket in her shoulder bag.

"What are you going to do?" Lao Ma asked after Pan-pan told him who she was and where she was bound. "I'll try to get you onto the next train to Beijing, but that won't be until tomorrow afternoon. As for your luggage, let's hope someone on the train turns it in to the authorities in Beijing. But I wouldn't count on it."

His caution made Pan-pan cry harder. All she had now was her shoulder bag and the soiled clothes on her back.

"I have no money for another ticket," she sobbed.

"You won't have to pay," Lao Ma replied. "I'll look after it. But you can't stay here all night. You need some rest. Why not come home with me after I finish my shift? My wife will be happy to meet you."

The stranger's kindness brought more tears to Pan-pan's eyes.

Lao Ma's wife, Lao Zhang, was waiting for them when they arrived at his home long after dark. Their two young sons had gone to bed. Pan-pan's head still ached, and her limbs were heavy with exhaustion. She had no appetite but, to be polite, she forced down the food she was served. At the end of the meal, Lao Zhang left the room, returning with a stack of clean garments and a towel.

"Have a soak in the tub if you like. It will make you feel better. There is plenty of hot water in the Thermos bottles. Use it all up," she suggested, pointing to a shed in the courtyard.

Pan-pan nodded and thanked Lao Zhang, then went out to the courtyard. The dimly lit bathroom closet had a squat toilet at one end and a brick sink at the other. A large wooden tub stood on its edge next to the sink. Pan-pan lowered the tub to the floor, pushed it under the tap, and turned on the water before pouring the hot water into it. As she began to unbutton her shirt, the familiarity of the routine reminded her of home—the tiny kitchen and … "and the powder," she hissed, turning to pick up her shoulder bag. Hastily rummaging through the bag, she found an unopened tin of powder, next to a half-empty bag of dried bread.

Pan-pan tested the bath water with her toe, and stepped into the tub. What a joke, she thought, shaking her head and staring into the rising steam. Of all the things she had once possessed, only the powder tin remained, like a faithful companion. But almost immediately she realized that she should be grateful, if not thankful, for having the powder with her. She would need it because she was about to spend the night with total strangers.

After she had bathed, Pan-pan put on the clothes Lao Zhang had lent her. The pants were the right length but the waist was far too large, so Pan-pan secured it with her own belt. The socks turned out to be brand new, thick at the bottom and soft against her bruised soles. But as she reached for the folded blouse, her hand stopped in midair. "I can't wear this," she said to herself. The constant warnings of Xin-Ma and Ah-Po rang in her ears. She might pass her fox smell to Lao Zhang. "It's just another silly old wives' tale," her father had said to her before she left home. But at the same time, both Ah-Po and Xin-Ma had sounded so certain of it. "No wind, no waves," Xin-Ma had argued. No matter what, Pan-pan concluded, she couldn't risk offending the woman who was being so kind to her.

Then another thought occurred to her. If she appeared in front of Lao Ma, Lao Zhang, and their sons the next day still wearing her own soggy, bloodstained shirt, she might as well have the words *fox smell* written on her forehead. How on earth could she avoid them asking questions? The agony of indecision was splitting her head into halves. She wished her mother were there, or even Xin-Ma, with her quick decisiveness.

Pressing her lips together, Pan-pan picked up the blouse. She would wash her own clothes first thing in the morning, at dawn. When they were dry, she would then wash Lao Zhang's garments and hope that her brief contact wouldn't contaminate them.

Later, lying alone on a cot in a small spare room, Pan-pan wished for the first time that she was back in her own bed, sharing the room with Ah-Po, with Xin-Ma and Gui-yang next door. But how would I tell them about the stolen money and the new clothes and the quilt I lost? she thought before falling into a troubled asleep.

When pan-pan woke up, it was almost noon, and the first thing that came to her mind was her unwashed laundry. Now what could she do? The house and the courtyard were quiet, so she got out of bed, put on her borrowed clothes, and entered the kitchen, where she found Lao Zhang seated at the table, a newspaper open before her.

"There you are," Lao Zhang said cheerily, taking off her glasses. "My goodness! Look at you. I had no idea I'd grown so big. My pants look like a skirt on you." She laughed, pointing toward the courtyard. "But don't worry. Your clothes were nearly dry last time I checked. Are you feeling a bit better today?"

"My clothes?" Pan-pan repeated silently, missing Lao Zhang's question. She stared out at the clothes hanging on a line in the sun and her eyes froze on her shirt whipping in the wind. She glanced at Lao Zhang, searching for any sign that she had noticed anything out of the ordinary when she washed Pan-pan's clothes.

"How are you feeling today?" Lao Zhang asked again.

"Oh, much better, I think. I'm sorry I slept in. You shouldn't have—" She stopped, pointing at the laundry.

"Don't mention it. I've got nothing else to do. You had a rough day. I'll get you some tea, then we'll eat."

Over a bowl of dumplings filled with stir-fried eggs and minced cabbage, Lao Zhang told Pan-pan that she had taken a day off from her new job as a thief-catcher in a nearby supermarket. "It was the only kind of work I could find after being laid off from the steel factory where I'd been a bookkeeper for over twenty years," she said bitterly. "The state-owned mill went bankrupt and closed down because of the government's new economic policies. So all of us workers have been thrown out on the street, jobless and penniless." According to Lao Zhang, the steel mill was once the pride of the city and the largest employer in the region. Not long ago, a wealthy businessman from Hong Kong had bought it and turned it into a recreation centre.

"Palace of Eternal Delight," Lao Zhang went on, shaking her head. "Who would have thought it? Where the furnaces used to stand, there's now a dance hall and bowling alleys. Where the steel was made and shaped, people now sing karaoke every night.

I won't last at this new job. It requires someone who has a heart of stone. I've been there for less than a month and already I've lost two days' pay for failing to report shoplifters. They were jamming food into their mouths—blackened bananas and stale buns—the kind of things most people wouldn't buy anyway. They were so desperate, in their shabby clothes, that I couldn't bring myself to stop them."

Wrapping her hands around her tea glass, Pan-pan sat gazing at the tabletop, listening to Lao Zhang out of politeness. She didn't understand some of the words and phrases and wondered why Lao Zhang was telling all this to a young woman she didn't even know. At first Pan-pan had thought the kindly woman might just be lonely. But it soon became clear that Lao Zhang had her own agenda. Sharing the worries and anxieties she had harboured for some time was her method of dissuading Pan-pan from continuing her trip to Beijing.

"Pan-pan, we'd be more than happy to buy you a ticket home," she said abruptly, and quickly added, "express class."

"Why would you want to do that, Lao Zhang? We're not even related."

"Because," Lao Zhang answered, lowering her eyes to her tea, "because I want you to set an example for my sons. They're only ten and twelve and already they've been talking about leaving Bengbu to work and live in larger cities."

"But I've never even spoken to your kids," Pan-pan said wearily. "It's not my fault if they want to go away."

"Of course not." Lao Zhang softened her voice, but kept frowning. "But it's madness again. You see, when I was a bit older than you are now, the government *forced* me to leave home, to live and work among total strangers. To be re-educated, as they called it, by peasants. I hated every minute of it. Now everyone, especially the younger ones, is eager to head for the cities. They think they can get rich there. But they'll all end up being as exploited and as lonely as I was."

As Lao Zhang clattered on, Pan-pan's mind drifted back to the sights at the train stations she had passed—the throngs of travellers, the different dialects humming inside the cars and outside on the platform, and, always, people seeing someone off or waiting to be taken somewhere. It seemed the entire population was on the move.

Now Lao Zhang was trying to talk her into abandoning her plan and returning home. Yet listening to what she had been saying only made Pan-pan realize that she had already missed plenty of opportunities and lagged far behind the rest of the country. Even Lao Zhang's young sons want to be part of the excitement, she reminded herself. I should at least give it a try. But how am I going to explain that to her? It will only disappoint her—and she's been treating me like her own child. As soon as Pan-pan heard Lao Ma's voice, she rushed out to greet him.

"Good news," he called out as he entered the courtyard.

Pan-pan followed him back inside.

"First things first," Lao Ma said, looking in a mirror to adjust his white cloth cap on his head. "Someone turned in your luggage to the station manager in Beijing. Second, I reported your situation to my leader. He's agreed to let you complete your journey without extra cost. That is, if you still want to." He glanced at his wife. "Or you can forget the whole thing. I'll arrange to have your luggage sent back here, and we'll be very glad to buy you a ticket home."

"Express class," Lao Zhang repeated, beaming.

"Thank you so much," said Pan-pan, her throat thick with emotion, "but—" She stopped, and her head bowed low before she looked up again. "But I have come this far already. On top of that, if Lao Zhang, Sun Ming, and millions of kids my age did what they had to years ago, travelling hundreds, even thousands, of kilometres away from home, I'd like to give it a try too."

"But it was different then, Pan-pan," Lao Zhang interrupted. "We were forced to go! We had no choice. But you do."

Choice. The word struck Pan-pan's ears like a beating gong. The last time she'd heard the same word spoken was in that bitter argument between her parents years ago. Mom had used it to rationalize her trip to Tongren, the trip that killed her. Was it really a good thing to have more than one choice? Pan-pan wondered, momentarily doubting herself.

"How about letting me get your luggage back here first," Lao Ma suggested. "It will take only a day or two. Meantime, you're welcome to stay with us and have more time to think the whole thing over. This afternoon, we can all go watch a soccer match at our sons' school. That's why I'm home early. The boys would love to meet you. What do you think?"

Suddenly, Pan-pan's throbbing head seemed worse, and she felt tired again. "All right. I'll think about it while my luggage is being returned. But if you don't mind, I'd like to lie down a bit and skip the game as well," she said weakly.

The next day, Pan-pan's headache was almost gone, and her customary energy had returned. After seeing her sons off to school, Lao Zhang insisted on taking Pan-pan sightseeing. Bengbu—the city of Clam Wharf—built on the south shore of the Hui River, turned out to be much bigger, noisier, and crowded than Tongren. Pan-pan was amazed to see that shops and restaurants lined both sides of the main downtown street. Half the goods displayed in the store windows she couldn't identify, especially the items covered with shiny buttons and keys, blinking and twinkling and glittering in broad daylight. There were stylish clothes in every direction she turned: dashing, colourful, but, most of all, strange. The prosperity and progress were a huge contrast to the life she had known. As she tagged along, at times lagging behind, she couldn't help wondering why Lao Zhang's sons wanted to go somewhere else.

As the morning whiled away, Pan-pan came to realize that Lao Zhang had another motive for taking her sightseeing. From time to time she stopped and pointed, making comments like a tour guide. "Look over there, Pan-pan, on the corner. See the woman who's selling tea-boiled eggs? She's not a local. She probably came here to find a good job, but look what happened: She ended up cooking and selling eggs on the street. Heaven knows where she goes to wash and where she sleeps at night."

Lao Zhang then pointed out a young woman leaning against a brick wall outside a store, with her hand outstretched. "See that? I'm sure she's from the countryside, too. How awful! She should be at home with her family instead of begging on the street."

By the time they stepped into Lao Zhang's courtyard, Pan-pan was wracked with self-doubt. What had happened in the past few days was more than she had experienced in her entire fifteen years. At home, everyone she knew, including her father, had assumed that her decision to leave home was because of her cursed fox smell, no matter what she had said about wanting to see the world beyond her village. Pan-pan had overheard Xin-Ma talking to her father. "Like mother, like daughter," she'd said. "If someday she wants to get the problem fixed, you can't stop her as you tried to do with her mother. And what's a better place than the nation's capital? It has proper hospitals and real doctors."

Was that why her father hadn't argued hard against her plan? Was he afraid if he tried he would only push her farther away and harden her decision—and cause another tragedy? Ah-Po must have harboured the same fear. After swallowing her original objections, she had been more than willing to dig out Sun Ming's address. Or were they all, like Lao Zhang, waiting for her to discover on her own that the outside world was a crueller place than she could handle?

The next morning, Pan-pan could feel the heat of the sun on her back as she headed toward the train station to collect her bag and bedroll. But as on the previous day, the sun soon got lost behind the haze. Around her the trees were coming into leaf and the pale yellow willow twigs dangled over the sidewalks as if to greet the morning pedestrians. The scene reminded Pan-pan of home, where the flowers had already been in bloom when she left.

Pan-pan was glad to be alone again, glad to be out of Lao Ma and Lao Zhang's house for a change, to be away from her lingering sense of awkwardness and embarrassment. The night before, when Pan-pan thought everyone had gone to bed, she had risen from her cot and crept out to the bathroom. Fearful that someone might hear her, she had closed the door before starting to wash Lao Zhang's blouse. But a few moments later, Lao Zhang had appeared outside the door.

"Don't worry about it, Pan-pan," she said quietly. "Leave that for tomorrow. We've bought a little washing machine. Go to sleep now."

Pan-pan stared down at her suds-covered hands. "I … I'm almost finished."

"All right," Lao Zhang replied. "But listen, Pan-pan. Don't ever let small things crush you. Lift up your head. No one is perfect in this world." Then she went back into the house.

Later, tossing and turning on the cot, going over and over Lao Zhang's words, Pan-pan sighed. Of course she knew. She knew from the morning she washed my clothes. And so did the boys. Is that why they were so silent each time she appeared, why they excused themselves so quickly from the dinner table? Lao Zhang said they were shy in front of strangers. Pan-pan wasn't so sure.

Pan-pan found Lao Ma in a small office at the station, jammed with desks, benches, and chairs. Phones were ringing, fingers tapping on the outside windows; both were ignored. There had been a few train delays, Lao Ma explained to her, but the passengers were too impatient and too demanding. He asked one of his co-workers to take Pan-pan to get her luggage from the storage room before he picked up a ringing phone. "Go back home. I'll see you tonight," he called out, covering the mouthpiece.

Pan-pan slung her bedroll over her shoulder, picked up her bag, and slowly lurched out of the station, making her way down the stairs. Lao Zhang had pressed a twenty-yuan note into Pan-pan's pocket, her taxi fare back to the house. But at the corner of the busy square, Pan-pan stopped and put down her bag and bedroll. Despite Lao Zhang's words of comfort and despite the fact that neither she nor Lao Ma had given any hint that they'd noticed her fox smell, Pan-pan was growing more anxious the more she thought about her problem. It was just a matter of time before their sons turned against her, a smelly stranger in their house. Besides, Pan-pan had no doubt that as soon as she walked through the door, Lao Zhang would start in on her again, urging her to return home.

In spite of all that had happened, Pan-pan felt she couldn't just slink back to the village of Western Clouds. For one thing, she would lose face; but more important, she wouldn't be able to live with herself if she threw away her dreams after one little bump in the road. Yes, she would carry on with her journey.

But she had no money, except the twenty-yuan taxi fare. Pan-pan let out another anguished sigh as she looked across the bustling square, at the people, the cars and buses, the ringing bicycles—all rushing to and fro with a purpose, a place to go, a destination to reach.

Chapter Eleven

With her bedroll as a cushion, Pan-pan sat leaning against the bottom step of the staircase leading to the train station. She closed her eyes, lifted her face toward the sun, and enjoyed the solitude, free at last from the talking, thinking, and unending self-consciousness of the past three days. She had been showered with enough metaphors, wise expressions, and quotations to last a lifetime.

A high-pitched voice, an accent she recognized, caused her eyes to pop open. Pan-pan sat up, searching for the source. No more than five metres from her stood a young woman wearing a heavy brown corduroy jacket, despite the humidity that had been looming over the city for the last couple of days. While the jacket hung loosely on her tiny frame, her pant legs ended inches above her plastic flip-flops. Pan-pan leaned forward for a better look. The young woman's face needed a good scrub, as Ah-Po would have said. But the discoloured patches on her cheeks were not dirt spots, nor birthmarks, Pan-pan realized. They were bruises. Her greasy hair dangled in strands, brushing her shoulders. Her accent, similar to that heard in Guizhou Province, placed her as a native of Sichuan, the province just to the northwest of Pan-pan's village.

She's about my age, probably a lonely traveller like me, Pan-pan said to herself. Yet the young woman had only a small bag with her, swinging weightlessly on her wrist. She was trying to stop a woman passerby.

"Auntie, could you tell me where I can buy a train ticket to Shanghai?"

"Shanghai?" The elder woman grimaced as if she had just swallowed a live worm. Tucking her purse deeper into her armpit, she snarled, "Don't come any closer! I know your type. One minute you're asking for information, the next you'll be gone with my money."

"You don't have to insult me," the young woman replied.

"Take a look at yourself," the woman kept on. "A ticket to Shanghai?" she chuckled. "You're about as believable as those beggars over there. You're young, and you have no missing arms or legs. Why can't you work to earn a living instead of fibbing and stealing?"

"Stealing?" the young woman shouted. "I'm not a thief, you old goat. And I've never cheated anyone in my life." She turned around, facing the small crowd that had formed around the two of them. "I have my own money. I'll show you if you don't believe me," she said, thrusting her hand into the cloth bag.

"Don't!" Pan-pan shouted as she jumped up and charged toward the gathering, thrusting one arm in front of her like a magic wand. "Don't take it out!"

OVER A GLASS OF TEA in a food stall behind the station, Pan-pan and Shui-lian sat and talked, ignoring the owner's scornful looks after they had repeatedly refused to order more drinks. Hours slipped by as they chatted. Morning rolled into noon. Sipping their tea and sharing a sweet bun, they exchanged their experiences, concluding that they had both been derailed on their way to their destinations, and their goals remained as far apart as the two cities they had intended to reach: Beijing to the north and Shanghai to the south.

But they seemed to draw strength from each other's stories, agreeing that neither should go back to her old life in the mountains or on the rivers.

"Not until I have found a job and made something of myself," Shui-lian said determinedly. "Something other than a river *ku-li.*"

"So why not come to Beijing with me? We can look for work together," Pan-pan replied, a smile appearing on her face as she set down her empty glass.

"Why don't *you* come with *me* to Shanghai?" Shui-lian countered.

"Beijing is the capital, so it's better."

"How do you know? You've never been there," Shui-lian demanded, her voice rising. "I heard that Shanghai is bigger and has a lot more people than Beijing—which to me means more factories and more job opportunities."

"Maybe so, but large or small, you don't know anyone there, while I have a connection in Beijing. Remember I told you about Sun Ming, the girl from Beijing, who was sent down to my village and lived with my family before she returned home? I have her address. We can look for her when we get to the capital, and she can help us find work."

Shui-lian burst out laughing. "You also told me all that happened about thirty years ago. Even if this Sun Ming still lives there, she may have forgotten your family. She certainly won't know you. You weren't even born yet!"

"That's true," Pan-pan answered calmly. "But, still, it's something. More than you've got in Shanghai."

Shui-lian fell quiet, avoiding Pan-pan's eyes as she thought for a moment. "It's not just that. I asked Jin-lin to tell my mother I was heading to Shanghai. What if—" She stopped, biting her lip.

"Sorry, I forgot that part. As far as my family knows, I'm already in Beijing," Pan-pan said bitterly. "Look at us: two warriors wounded already, before the battle is launched. Anyway, even if I was willing to go to Shanghai with you, I don't have the money for a train ticket." She pulled some money from her pocket. "This is all I have left, and it belongs to Lao Zhang. My taxi fare. Lao Ma's explained to me that I have two options. One, to accept a free ticket to Beijing; the other, to let them pay my way back home. You know what, Shui-lian? Either way is a sort of dead end because I have no money. It was all stolen. What will I do if I can't find Sun Ming in Beijing? I'll be totally alone in a strange city."

"You're not backing out, taking their offer, are you?" Shui-lian sounded more worried than alarmed. She had been talking tough, making it seem that her mind was made up about Pan-pan going to Shanghai with her. The truth was that, after her short encounter with Pan-pan, she didn't just like this easygoing and level-headed young woman—who was, Shui-lian thought, the kind of daughter her own mother would have wished for—Shui-lian felt she could trust Pan-pan. She knew she had found a friend in this young woman from a neighbouring province. Of course, she would never share everything with her as she did with Jin-lin, she cautioned herself, especially the account of her rape on that horrible night. She would tell Pan-pan about being abducted by a gang that sold women into forced marriages, and about being arrested and released, but no more.

"No, I'm not backing out," Pan-pan assured Shui-lian but without much conviction. Time was running out, she reminded herself. She had to make a decision one way or the other, and soon.

After the food stall owner glowered at them again and shooed them away, Pan-pan suggested they walk and talk some more to clear their heads. "But let's avoid the area around the train station," she added. "Lao Ma must be looking for me by now. He and his wife are probably worried that something has happened to me." She then stopped, lowering her head as if making a confession. "I'm grateful for their help, but I can't deliver what they want." She straightened the criss-cross tie on her bedroll before slinging it onto her back. "I feel like if I refuse to go home as they wish, I'll be throwing ashes in their faces in return for the sack of coal they gave me to save me from freezing to death. You understand what I'm saying, don't you?"

"Of course I do. I went to school too, you know," Shui-lian said defensively as she picked up Pan-pan's bag. Although she didn't quite get the ashes and coal part, the meaning was clear. Listening to Pan-pan talk about Lao Ma and Lao Zhang and their kindness toward her, a stranger, Shui-lian couldn't help feeling a little envious.

"I bet Comrade Guo was disappointed as well when she returned to the inn and found out that I'd left on my own despite her advice. She offered to buy me a train ticket home. Probably also express class," Shui-lian felt compelled to say. Yet, in spite of Guo and her sympathetic words, Shui-lian didn't share Pan-pan's belief in the essential kindness of people. Da-Ge and the men who had raped her, Jin-lin, and the others had made that impossible.

A MAN'S VOICE came out of nowhere as Pan-pan and Shui-lian were about to cross a busy intersection. "Are you looking for work, young misses?"

Shui-lian started, panic in her eyes. Pan-pan quickly reached out to catch Shui-lian by the arm before her friend lurched into the path of an oncoming truck. Pan-pan was still laughing at Shui-lian's reaction when she turned around to see the man who was the cause of the commotion. She looked up into a pair of friendly eyes behind thick spectacles.

"I'm very sorry if I startled you," the man apologized, smiling and revealing gaps between his upper teeth, which explained the hissing sound like leaking valves that Pan-pan had heard when he spoke. His politeness and gentle voice put Pan-pan at ease right away. He was about Ah-Po's age, tall, lanky, and slightly stooped, and his face was a map of folds and creases.

"Old Uncle, were you talking to us?" she asked.

"Don't say anything to him!" Shui-lian insisted. "And don't call him 'uncle'! He's a wolf in a lamb's coat! Let's go!" She grabbed Pan-pan's arm.

"Stop! You're hurting me!" Pan-pan protested loudly, struggling to free herself. "What's the matter with you, Shui-lian? I want to hear what he has to say. For heaven's sake, what are you afraid of?

It's broad daylight and there are hundreds of people on the street. Besides, there are two of us. He can't eat us alive, can he?"

"You're making a mistake, Pan-pan. You can't get ivory from the mouth of a dog. Men are all the same. All they do is tell lies and trick you," Shui-lian grumbled, reluctantly releasing Pan-pan's arm. "A pig's fart will smell a hundred times better than whatever comes out of his mouth!"

"What a temper! What a way to talk!" The old man said in a trembling voice, visibly shaken. "Why don't you listen to what I have to say before you run out of animals to insult me with?"

Shui-lian glared at him, her chest heaving.

"I don't like to chase after strangers on the street, especially young women, but I'm just doing my job."

He took off his khaki cap, using his open palm to smooth a head of white hair. "I recruit workers for a shoe factory on the northern outskirts of Bengbu. The factory won't hire me to work there because I'm too old to be productive. My hands are slow and my eyesight is poor. It's only interested in young people, young women in particular. And only non-locals."

"I've never made shoes," Pan-pan answered, her voice trailing. Turning to Shui-lian she said behind her hand, "Remember what we've talked about? We need money." Back to the old man, she patted the bedroll on her back and the bag slung across Shui-lian's shoulder and added, "You can see yourself that we're not locals. Will you hire us?"

"Don't listen to him!" Shui-lian jerked her head, facing Pan-pan, her voice cracking and pleading. "That's how they all start, making job offers because that's what you want to hear. I know what I'm talking about. They'll promise you the moon and the sun, anything to hook you."

She swung around to challenge the old man, her eyes boring into his. "If you want us to believe you, you'd better take us to the factory yourself."

To Shui-lian's surprise, a smile reappeared on the old man's face, bringing more creases around his eyes. "I'm happy to oblige your request. But first, let's find a quiet place to sit down so that I can tell you more about it. I've been on my feet since the crack of dawn. Please keep in mind," he paused, casting a long glance of disfavour at Shui-lian, "I'm going to ask you some questions, and I have to be satisfied with the answers before I can sign you up for the job."

AN HOUR LATER, the interview, held in a snack bar over bottles of orange pop for Pan-pan and Shui-lian and a glass of beer for himself, was concluded. Forms had been filled in and, most important, Shui-lian's doubts and fears had been calmed by the old man's reassurances, and by the fact that they would be travelling to the factory on a public bus, with other passengers. The recruiter, who asked the girls to call him Lao Zhou, walked Pan-pan and Shui-lian to the city's long-distance bus station and waited in line with them for tickets. Outside there was a constant coming and going of vehicles, and jostling crowds. Tickets in hand, Shui-lian and Pan-pan joined another line in a sheltered area. Lao Zhou, who, it turned out, was a retired middle-school history teacher, motioned Shui-lian aside, out of earshot of the other passengers.

In a hushed voice he reminded her that at no time should she tell anyone in the factory that she was from Sichuan. She and Pan-pan must pretend to be cousins, on her mother's side, as he'd written on their employment forms. Earlier, during the interview, Lao Zhou had emphasized that the owner of the factory, a wealthy businesswoman from Taiwan who now lived in the United States with her American husband, was said to dislike Sichuan natives. One rumour had it that her discontent was rooted in her unhappy family history. Another claimed that years ago she had had a similar factory outside the city of Suzhou but had shut it down because of, in her words, "the high cost of land and taxes and dwindling profits." The truth was, Lao Zhou whispered, the workers there had tried to organize a union, demanding higher pay and benefits.

"Benefits?" Shui-lian had asked, frowning. "What are they? The workers were paid, weren't they? What else did they want that made the boss so mad she closed the factory?"

"I'm not sure about the details. The reason I'm bringing it up is that the labour dispute was initiated by a group of migrant workers from Sichuan. Before you knew it, everyone came on board. As a group they requested better living and working conditions, and some medical coverage. As you may know, the once-proud universal medicare run by our government went down the drain long ago. The owner accused the workers of getting fancy ideas from the West." Lao Zhou raised one of his eyebrows, producing a funny face. "Did I tell you that every pair of shoes made in the factory is for foreign markets only? Anyway, I'm not allowed to sign on any workers from Sichuan Province."

He looked straight at Shui-lian, who stared back at him as she wiped cookie crumbs off her lips. He then wiggled his first finger at her. "After what I've experienced today, I can't blame her too much, can I?" Not waiting for an answer, he threw back his head and let out a heartfelt laugh. "Little Sichuan, you sure are a firecracker."

As the last of the passengers rushed to take their seats, Lao Zhou stood on his toes on the platform so he was at eye level with Pan-pan and Shui-lian, who had taken seats next to an open window. He lowered his voice, giving them his final advice. "Look out for yourself and for each other when you are there. Watch what you say, and stay out of trouble. China may still call itself a socialist country, ruled by the Communist Party, but it's capitalism inside the factory walls. Remember: When you live in someone else's house, bend your head if the ceiling is lower than what you're used to."

His last words released a gush of homesickness in Shui-lian. Her mother had often used the same saying. For the past two days, ever since she had left Jin-lin and the other women at the inn, she had been up with the rising sun, walking and begging all day, sleeping in shabby hostels, where she paid three yuan a night for a top bunk. For two days she had thought about nothing but her destination—Shanghai—and starting a new life there. It had been hard to keep her mind off her mother and her family, the rivers and mountains of Sichuan, but she knew she had to, otherwise her will might soften, and she might break down right in the middle of road and give up her plan.

As the bus rumbled out of the station, Shui-lian wondered where Jin-lin was. She found herself choked with emotions she thought she had lost forever after that horrible night. Quickly she turned her head aside, away from the window. She didn't want Pan-pan to see her tears.

Chapter Twelve

The bus rattled and grumbled, heading north. Pan-pan sat quietly, a ten-yuan note crumpled in her fist. She had tried to push the money into Lao Zhou's hand when he shook hands with her before the bus pulled out of the station, but failed. She knew it would cover only part of the bus fare, but it was all the money she had left. Ordinarily, the workers bought their own tickets and were repaid by the factory once they passed their three-month probation. But Lao Zhou was kind enough to buy her and Shui-lian's tickets for them. Pan-pan stared down at the wrinkled note in her hand, feeling a thickness in her throat. She wondered whether by the end of the day, week, or month, the old man would ever break even, never mind earning money as he hoped, if he kept helping out people like her and Shui-lian.

Next to her, Shui-lian, gazing at the back of the seat in front of her, spoke quietly. "I never said goodbye to my family, nor did I wave at anyone during the entire trip, even though we were constantly in and out of trains and on and off buses." She looked out the window as if retracing her journey. "But saying goodbye to Lao Zhou, someone I had just met, made me sad. It's very strange, but you know what? I kind of like it—it's a good sad-feeling."

Pan-pan didn't reply.

According to Lao Zhou, the bus ride to the factory was about three hours. It would take them to the north shore of the Hui River and onto the North China Plain, where Anhui Province bordered Henan Province. Although the factory was less than a year old, Lao Zhou said, a bus stop had already been set up and named after it. "A stone's throw from the factory," he assured them. "Trust me, you won't miss it."

It turned out that six other young women on the bus were heading for the same destination. "The new shoemakers," the driver had called them.

The bus was jammed full. Every seat was taken, including the flip-downs that blocked the centre aisle. Bags and parcels filled up the remaining space—piled on the overhead racks, heaped on raised knees, and enclosed by anxious arms. Two galvanized-wire cages sat on top of the engine cover. One held half a dozen scrawny chickens, the other a pair of ducks that seemed in better spirits than the chickens, quacking and flapping their wings each time the bus horn sounded.

As the sun slanted down the western sky, Pan-pan and Shui-lian experienced their first traffic jam while the bus fought its way out of Bengbu. They laughed at the chaos outside the window, the noise, the tangled disorder among the vehicles, cyclists, and pedestrians, and the loud curses from their driver. When the bus finally reached the countryside, the daylight was fading and the relative calm seemed to bring quiet among the riders. Animated conversations, carried on in several dialects, each louder than the other, had diminished to hushed murmurs and soft snores.

Shui-lian dozed off, her head on the bedroll Pan-pan had placed on her knees. It's probably the first time she's had a decent rest since she left her family's boat more than a week ago, Pan-pan thought as she watched a trickle of saliva gather at the corner of Shui-lian's mouth. Shui-lian had told her about Da-Ge's lies and betrayal, her troubled journey, that she had almost been sold as a wife to a stranger. Pan-pan couldn't have imagined that such terrible things happened. Listening to Shui-lian's story, Pan-pan had felt guilty about her own so-called adversity. She wondered if she would have chosen to return home like the rest of the women Shui-lian had travelled with. Shui-lian was so brave, Pan-pan admitted. Yet taking off without telling her family was something she herself would never do.

With Shui-lian sleeping soundly, Pan-pan leaned closer to examine her face in the dim light. Although Pan-pan was four months younger and less experienced, she concluded that the bruises on Shui-lian's face were definitely not from falling down the stairs as Shui-lian had claimed. More likely she had been punched. Did something else happen during her trip that Shui-lian didn't want to tell me? Pan-pan asked herself. If so, does it cancel out my not revealing my fox smell? No wonder Lao Zhou called us *nan-jie-nan-mei*—suffering sisters—after he finished listening to the edited version of our stories.

Pan-pan knew that the popular expression was actually *nan-xiong-nan-di*—suffering brothers. Whoever came up with that old proverb seemed to imply that misery falls only on males. Xin-Ma would have said that was because it was always men who made up words and phrases. Then again, Lao Zhou used to be a teacher. He knew how to reinvent phrases. Is that why he took pity on us, two suffering young women, and signed us on by lying about Shui-lian's birthplace and paying for our tickets? As soon as they, especially Shui-lian, were convinced that Lao Zhou wasn't a phoney and his job offer was real, they had both tried to persuade, even pleaded for, the old man to hire them. No matter how tough the job turned out to be, they promised not to complain. Anything would be better than the situation back at home, and working in a factory seemed the only way for them to escape poverty and humiliation.

The bus rolled along in the twilight, letting passengers off and taking more on board. Pan-pan closed her eyes, trying to imagine what her worker's life would be like. She had never made shoes for herself. How could she make shoes for foreigners? She'd be able to support herself, although Lao Zhou didn't know exactly how much she'd earn. He did mention that the cost of water, electricity, and living quarters, including the rental of bunk beds, would be deducted from their monthly pay. And the workers were responsible for their own meals. If expenses were too high, maybe she and Shui-lian could share one bed. Instinctively, Pan-pan pressed her arms tight against her side. On second thought, it would be better if she slept by herself. Maybe she could save money on food instead.

"Niavia Station. Shoemakers, your stop," the driver called out, switching on the ceiling lights. The bus made a tight turn and stopped in the middle of a narrow road thronged with people. A streetlight cast its glare upon the crowd. The din and smells hanging thickly in the air could be grabbed by the fistful. No sooner had the bus come to a stop than the door flapped open and hands appeared outside the windows, thrusting and waving in the air like tentacles. Shui-lian jerked awake and bumped her head on the window sill. She rubbed her eyes and stretched her arms, then stopped in the middle of a yawn when her sleepy eyes caught sight of the hustle and bustle outside. Pan-pan was already up on her feet, also yawning. The last time she had looked out the window, the bus was travelling through serene farmers' fields, earth and sky merged into a murky vastness.

Gingerly, Pan-pan, Shui-lian, and the six other recruits climbed down the steps, clutching their belongings tightly against their chests, their eyes shifting from side to side as they took in the intimidating commotion. Pan-pan hung onto her bedroll. Shui-lian huddled uneasily behind Pan-pan, protected by the bulky bag at her side.

As soon as the bus took off, before the trail of dust settled back to the ground, all eight newcomers were encircled by a wall of strangers and immersed in a sea of bellowing voices. Each hawker tried to top the next, urging the new workers, or "money bags" as they insisted on calling them, to purchase the best goods that money could buy and to sit down for the most delicious meal they would ever eat. Colourful dresses and blouses were waved in their faces. Pan-pan leaped to the side like a startled frog when she realized that someone was kneeling at her feet, attempting to snatch her leg.

"Get away from me!" she screamed. "What do you want?"

A tiny face looked up. A boy smiled at her, his front teeth missing. "Let me clean your shoes." He pointed at Pan-pan's mud-caked running shoes with their mismatched laces. "Cheap, Big Sister. One yuan per foot."

Behind her, Shui-lian was fighting a much fiercer battle, struggling to free herself from fingers grabbing at her hair. One woman persistently shoved a picture torn from a magazine into Shui-lian's face. "The newest hair style," she crowed. "Only twenty yuan."

Everyone seemed to be yelling. No one was listening or taking no for an answer. Shui-lian covered her head with Pan-pan's bag. Around them, the other recruits were waging similar fights, breaking free from a tangle of intruding arms. If it were not for the arrival of Mr. Yao, Pan-pan was sure some of them would have ended up missing a limb or two. As soon as the short, bulky man barged into the melee, the crowd became quiet, as if someone had turned a knob and switched off the radio.

Mr. Yao introduced himself as the manager of the Department of People's Affairs for the Niavia Shoe Company. "At least he isn't calling himself Da-Ge or boss man," Shui-lian whispered into Pan-pan's ear.

Mr. Yao wore a pink shirt buttoned up to his chin, set off by a butterfly-shaped tie made from gold ribbon. Pan-pan could tell right away that the thick hair on his round head wasn't his own. The wig had shifted to the left when he butted triumphantly into the crowd. As Mr. Yao and his assistant busied themselves shooing away the vendors, Pan-pan kept her eyes on his toupee. It reminded her of the metal lid her father had made for the water pot on the brick stove.

After a quick head count and roll call, Mr. Yao adjusted his frameless glasses, which kept sliding down his nose, and led the recruits away. By now the crowd had dispersed, but their jeers rose from both sides of the road as the young women passed. Someone mimicked rooster crows, followed by quacks of ducks as another voice called out, "Look! Such a flock of pretty ducklings. Look! An ugly rooster leading them."

Shui-lian and Pan-pan trudged behind Mr. Yao, their eyes drawn to the ramshackle stores and food stalls, most of them set up under large tarpaulins, tied to the dust-coated trees and posts. Strings of cooked meat and chickens with their heads still on dangled upside down inside dimly lit food stands. Tables and benches were set out along the edge of the dirt road. Steam hung over large pots resting on coal stoves, filling the evening air with coal dust and savoury aromas and reminding the two girls how hungry they were. Nearby, men and women shouted in competition, selling cooked eggs, deep-fried bean curd, and roasted melon seeds.

"This must be the market Lao Zhou told us about," Shui-lian whispered. The old recruiter had mentioned that the market had popped up right after the factory opened and had been expanding ever since. The farmers-turned-merchants called the workers their *yao-qian-shu*—money trees. The factory stood in the middle of farmland and the closest city, Bozhou, was thirty kilometres to the west. Since the factory workers had only one day off every two weeks, the locals grabbed every opportunity they could to make money from the "members of the salaried class."

Chapter Thirteen

The Niavia Shoe Company was virtually hidden from the outside world behind a high red-brick wall, on top of which fragments of glass poked skyward from the mortar, reflecting the glare of the perimeter lights. A tall cast-iron gate marked the entrance, while a sturdy guardhouse stood next to it. Inside, Shui-lian, Pan-pan, and the rest of the recruits followed Mr. Yao along a dirt path and onto a paved road that wound between large, featureless warehouse-style buildings of grey concrete. At the back of the compound, rows of one-storey shacks with whitewashed walls and dark roof tiles stood in rigid columns like soldiers at attention. A wide ditch divided the shacks into two uneven blocks. These long, narrow buildings, Mr. Yao announced, were the workers' dorms. There were seventy of them altogether, housing about eight hundred workers—five hundred female and three hundred male. Tin-roofed shelters, only one for each block, served as washing areas. "Left side men, right side women," Mr. Yao asserted.

The farmers had nicknamed the compound "Nightmares of the Red Mansion" after the Chinese classic novel *Dreams of Red Mansions.* They were bitter and angry at the factory's refusal to hire local residents. The owner, Gong-Da-Xiao-Jie—Elder Miss Gong—claimed that to run a "tight ship," outsiders were best.

From her experience, she had concluded that the farther her workers were from their hometowns, the less chance they would quit, and the less chance still that the locals would get involved in what was going on inside the factory. A stranded ship, some called the factory, because at the foot of the outside wall a ten-metre-wide moat had been dug through the fields of wheat, millet, and vegetables. This design had further enraged the local elders, who accused the owner of making a mockery of the Forbidden City in Beijing, the home of China's emperors for centuries. It, too, was surrounded by a moat as a defence against attack.

Eleven months after the factory began production and after nearly a million pairs of Niavia-brand running shoes had been shipped across the Pacific, no one in the factory had yet laid eyes on the powerful Elder Miss Gong, although her edicts kept floating down like dandruff, reminding the workers from the moment they opened their eyes in the morning that "We must make more shoes." Her latest decree had been written on large red cotton sheets hung above the pathways, printed on colourful paper pasted on the walls of the canteen and toilets, and repeated over and over by Mr. Tony and Mr. Tom each time they moved their lips, it seemed. Mr. Tony and Mr. Tom were Elder Miss Gong's American assistants, or her left and right arms, as they proudly called themselves. Her two furry arms, said the workers behind the men's backs, because their forearms were covered with thick black hair.

Following Mr. Yao's directions, the new workers were shown to their assigned dorms. Pan-pan and Shui-lian were taken to Dorm Number 12, a concrete cell about three metres wide and eight metres long, with tiny windows along the top of the side walls. Shui-lian was instantly reminded of the blockhouses she had seen from time to time up on the riverbanks, remnants of China's civil wars. Six double bunks were lined against the bare cement walls, three on one side of the room and three on the other. A single bare bulb burned feebly at the end of a wire a few centimetres below the ceiling, struggling to illuminate the cramped room and its inhabitants. The air was stale, damp, and musty.

All the top bunks were taken. Since there were no chairs and no room for any other furniture, most of the occupants were sitting on the beds, leaning against their rolled-up bedding, chatting or nibbling snacks. In the narrow aisle running down the centre of the room, two young women stood on the hard-packed dirt floor, facing each other in their panties and tank tops and arguing heatedly, their hands flying rapidly about in the air. Their shouting was brought to an abrupt halt by the arrival and stern voice of Elder Sister Meng, the director of the Sewing Department.

Meng then did a quick introduction, calling out the name of each occupant in the room. Before she turned to leave, she pointed out two vacant lower bunks next to the door, across from each other, and told Shui-lian and Pan-pan that they'd better hurry and unpack their belongings because the light would go out in less than an hour.

Pan-pan began to untie her bedroll and insisted over Shui-lian's protests that Shui-lian take the new quilt Pan-pan had been given by Xin-Ma. She could make do with a sheet and her cotton-padded jacket until Shui-lian got her own.

"What are you? A diehard Communist?" a woman who was half-lying and half-sitting on the top bunk above Pan-pan sneered, even though her mouth was jammed full of food. "If your pal doesn't want your quilt, I wouldn't mind—"

"Who do you think you are?" Shui-lian cut her off fiercely. "Get your own damn quilt!"

"My, my, my." The woman pulled herself up and swung her legs over the edge of the bed, her eyes narrowed to slits. "Maybe I should come down and teach you some manners."

"Stop it, Shui-lian," Pan-pan cried out. "Give me a hand, will you? Do you have to pick a fight with everyone you meet? Please forgive her," she pleaded with the woman in a shaky voice. "We had a long day. We are both tired."

The truth was, the cramped dorm alone was frightening enough without Shui-lian's outburst. Until the night she stayed with Lao Ma's family, Pan-pan had never lived with strangers. Although the prospect of an independent worker's life had excited her, suddenly not knowing what it comprised scared her just as much. She was nervous as it was, without a looming conflict.

"Remember Lao Zhou's final warning, or you're on your own," Pan-pan hissed at Shui-lian through clamped teeth. Forcing a smile, she quickly added, "Cousin."

"Cousin?" A woman whose name was Fang-yuan cut in, her slippers dragging as she approached Pan-pan. "Are you saying you two are related?" she demanded, tilting her head, her eyes moving back and forth as though spinning an invisible yarn between Pan-pan and Shui-lian.

"Yes, Fang-yuan Jie-Jie. On my mother's side," Pan-pan answered calmly. "She's Shui-lian, and I'm Pan-pan."

"Knock that grin off your face," Fang-yuan bellowed, her hands resting on her bony hips. Around her, up and down the aisle, all the chatter stopped. Faces turned toward the two newcomers. A couple of the women got off their beds and moved closer, anticipating a showdown.

Red faced, Fang-yuan continued, her voice quivering with anger. "In the past ten months, I've tried over and over to get the factory to hire my cousin, but time and again I failed. You know why?" She paused, glaring at Pan-pan. "I was told that the factory doesn't like relatives working together. Or in their exact words, 'When village clans get together, they cause trouble.'" She took a deep breath. "Village clans," she repeated and spat loudly onto the floor. "As if we're cavemen and -women. The irony is that my cousin no longer lives in a village because it was washed away by the great flood two years ago. She lost her entire family. She would have been dead too if she hadn't been visiting us when it happened. The last I heard, she had gone south to look for work after Niavia rejected her again, and I don't know where she is now."

All of a sudden she thrust her face directly in front of Pan-pan's. "I know the real reason," she jeered, spitting again, this time narrowly missing Pan-pan's foot. "Because I don't have a pretty face like yours, and I don't know how to fling cheap smiles around like used goods in a second-hand store and—"

"And?" Shui-lian snarled, stepped in between them, her face so close to the woman's that she felt the hot air flare out of her nostrils. "Cheap or not, at least they're smiles. I wonder if you could ever crack a sliver on that stiff board of yours. You'd better untwist your pinched face before someone does it for you."

"Stop! Stop it, both of you," Pan-pan shouted, slapping her thigh in frustration. "Fang-yuan, I'm sorry your cousin isn't here, but you can't blame us, can you?"

The belligerent woman's anger seemed to disappear. "I guess not," she admitted, shrugging her shoulders.

At that moment, a bell rang. "Come on, Fang-yuan. Curfew in ten minutes," someone called out.

Pan-pan silently spread her sheet on the wooden boards of her bunk. Still upset with her friend and refusing to look at her, she covered her upper body with her jacket and settled down just before the light went out.

An hour later, wrapped in pitch darkness, Pan-pan lay on her side, face to the wall, waiting anxiously for sleep to come. From a distance she heard the slap of flip-flops beating rhythmically on a pathway, growing louder until they stopped outside her dorm. Her eyes snapped open and her breath caught in her throat when she smelled the cigarette smoke that forced its way through the cracks of the plank door. A sharp clink and clunk echoed in the night air, followed by the rasp of a sliding bolt and the piercing slap of the hasp. Recognizing the noises, especially the clapping shut of a padlock, Pan-pan was seized by panic. She raised herself up to rest on her elbows. The slaps of the flip-flops resumed, moving toward the next dorm. Pan-pan began to tremble.

"Shui-lian," she whispered in a shaking voice.

"Yes, I'm awake."

"Shui-lian, we've been locked in!"

"I know."

Why is she so calm? Pan-pan thought with a surge of annoyance. What if there's a fire? Surely Shui-lian should know that only animals are treated in such a way. Pan-pan recalled her first visit, when she was five years old, to the village barn where three cows were kept at night.

"Why do we lock them up?" she had asked her mother. "They won't be able to get out if there's a fire." Her mother had explained that because good cows were expensive and hard to get, the villagers felt they had to apply double diligence to protect them. "I'm sure that if the cows could secure the door themselves from the inside, there'd be no need to lock them up at night," her mother had joked.

Early the next day, Pan-pan nervously headed for the public washing station that served the needs of nearly five hundred women. Dozens of taps projected from a naked pipe, suspended horizontally over a long cement sink, that dominated the centre area. The place was already crowded and noisy, alive with clatter and arguments and bodies jostling for access to the sink. Those who were tall like Pan-pan or strong could easily win a spot, hunching over the edge of the sink. Those who were small had to fight their way in, fill their washbasins, then carry them to the side and put them down on the floor. At one end of the building, a row of showerheads poked out of the rough grey wall, appearing lonely and aloof.

From the moment Pan-pan stepped into the washing area she was filled with dread, wondering how she could possibly carry out Ah-Po's instructions. She clutched her shoulder bag, hiding the tin of white powder, as her eyes wandered from one corner to another, searching in vain for a private spot. She doubted if Ah-Po's present would ever see light again. If not, it would be only a matter of days before her flaw was exposed. When she left home, she had looked forward to a new beginning. Now it seemed the adventure was about to rip open her secret, which she had kept even from her new friend, fearing public ridicule.

Down at the far end of the sink she saw Shui-lian, who, being shorter than most of the other women, tried to shove her way in to reach a tap. Already Pan-pan longed for the privacy of her home.

Back in the dorm, Pan-pan found herself alone with the dorm leader, a woman from southern Anhui. She confided to Wang-Jie—Sister Wang—her worries about the door being locked at night and related the story of her childhood visit to the barn. Sister Wang shrugged her shoulders and pressed her lips together, forming a thin line.

"Your mother sounds like a smart woman, but her explanation doesn't apply here. You would think there was a difference between animals and human beings, that the latter are the superior ones, wouldn't you? Trust me, girl. Just wait a week or two. You'll be like the rest of us, too tired to lift your eyelids. As soon as your head hits your pillow you'll hear nothing, see nothing, and be bothered by nothing. Lock or no lock."

"But it still doesn't mean we should be treated that way, sleeping or not sleeping. We're not animals!"

"Mind your manners, girl. Since you're talking about animals and people in one breath, let me tell you something. In many parts of the world, including China, some animals are treated much better than people. If you're not happy here and don't want to be locked up, you know where the door is."

It took Pan-pan a couple of seconds to realize what the dorm leader was implying. Frustrated and speechless, she returned to her bunk, silently picked up her enamel bowls, and headed to the canteen. Sister Wang's harsh words spun around in her head as she ate her rice porridge and steamed buns stuffed with pickled cabbage slices, surrounded by slurping and smacking noises. *Why is Sister Wang so nasty? It's totally uncalled for. She sounds so bitter and unhappy—yet she did praise my mom, calling her a smart woman.*

Thinking about Mom, Pan-pan unconsciously clenched her arms tightly against her ribcage, her eyes darting nervously about her as though someone out there could see what she was thinking or, worse, pick up the smell she was attempting to conceal. *How come Lao Zhou, the recruiter, who had told them so much about this factory, had failed to mention that attending to personal needs was a group activity, that washing and cleaning oneself was so open, like at a town fair?*

Chapter Fourteen

On their way to report to work after breakfast, Pan-pan told Shui-lian about her encounter with Sister Wang. Shui-lian listened and nodded a couple of times. But to Pan-pan's great disappointment and surprise, her friend responded lightheartedly, "I don't mind being locked up. It's better this way." Pointing to the rows of buildings on the other side of a litter-strewn trench, she then added, "You know who sleeps there, don't you? No-good-goddamn men. As far as I am concerned, no padlock is large enough to keep us safe from them."

At the entrance to the Sewing Department, where all eight new recruits were assigned, Shui-lian stood still, staring wide-eyed at the scene before her. Dust hung in humid air ripe with the sweat and strong body odours left behind by the departed night-shift workers. Until then, she had never set foot inside a factory. Nor had she been in such a large building. It reminded her of the huge cargo ships that lined Chongqing harbour. The pale morning light poured into the vast room through a row of high windows, illuminating lines of fluorescent tubes that dangled, buzzing and flaring, above row after row of strange-looking machines. Shui-lian couldn't help wondering if the department stores across China had ever run out of sewing machines.

According to Elder Sister Meng, sewing was the biggest department in the factory—larger than Cutting, Insole Making, or General Assembly. It employed over four hundred workers. Most were from the countryside, and all were female, some as young as fifteen and none older than thirty, except the director. Production continued around the clock. The workers were divided into two twelve-hour shifts—days, beginning at 7 A.M., and nights at 7 P.M. Every two weeks they got Sunday off, then they changed shifts. The owner's edict, *ren-ting-ji-bu-ting*—people stop, but not the machines—written in black ink brushed on red cloth and coloured paper, cried out from the walls of the compound, the canteens, and even the toilet rooms. Shui-lian would soon learn that in reality the machines would quit from time to time when they broke down, but the affected workers moved to other machines and kept going with no break.

The strange sights and noise started to unnerve Shui-lian. She turned to look for Pan-pan and the other new workers, only to find that all of them had been led away deeper into the shop by their trainers. A surge of panic struck Shui-lian. She decided to wait outside the door for her trainer, as Elder Sister Meng had instructed the night before. But her retreat was blocked by the stream of incoming workers. Angry shouts rose about her and irritable hands pushed her out of their way, until she was shoved to a corner with her back pressed against the cool concrete wall, watching throngs of young women frantically clocking in for the day shift.

Minutes later, Fang-yuan appeared silently in front of Shui-lian, a meaningful grin on her face. She pointed with her chin to the shop where the workers were dispersing furiously to their workstations, like water flowing downstream. Shui-lian shut her eyes and moaned. Over two hundred people in the workshop and she had to fall into the hands of this woman, who, in less than twelve hours since they met, already harboured a grudge against her. What luck on her first day in the factory! It was her mother who used to say that foes often met on a narrower path.

"Are you coming with me or not?" said Fang-yuan. "I won't bite you. But don't expect me to be nice to you. Remember, it was you who told me I'm unable to crack a smile."

Shui-lian opened her mouth; words lingered on her lips, but at the last minute she decided to hold them back.

Fang-yuan took the lead, stopping in front of a sewing machine in the far right-hand corner of the room. Once again she used her chin to do the talking, indicating the stool. Then she walked away. Shui-lian remained standing, taking in the features of the machine mounted on a wide plank before her: the countless knobs and dials, hooks, wires, the wheels and belt. The long, sharp needle reflected in the sunlight that streamed in through the window, aloof and threatening, posing a silent challenge. She looked around and saw that the black bins placed on each side of the machine were nearly full. The one on the left was filled with stacks of white fabric pieces shaped like flattened fish. They must be the lining of the shoe uppers, Shui-lian reminded herself, recalling the brief lesson given by Elder Sister Meng the night before. But the contents of the bin on the right were puzzling. The bin was divided into small compartments, each packed with leather meticulously cut into squares, triangles, rhomboids, large and small disks, and long and short strips. Their shapes resembled the popular tangram game of her childhood, which she had loved to play by herself. But unlike the tangram, with its seven differently coloured pieces, here all the cuts were white. Shui-lian reached down and picked up a long narrow segment. It had a gentle inward curve like a crescent moon and felt soft between her fingertips. She held it up to her nose, delighted by its faint scent of oil and sweetness.

"Put that down." Fang-yuan's voice came from behind her back. Shui-lian dropped the piece onto the pile and stood with her hands at her sides. "Don't touch anything unless I say so," Fang-yuan continued harshly. "In case no one has told you, each piece, no matter how small, is real leather, and worth what you or I make in a day. That is, when you're able to sew twenty-two of them in half an hour."

"You mean in a day, don't you?" said Shui-lian.

"Wrong. I mean half an hour. Twenty-two pieces make up just one shoe, and you and everyone else in the shop are expected to finish at least twenty shoes in each shift. Is that clear?"

Not waiting for a reply, Fang-yuan walked back to her machine and returned with a finished shoe upper, which she handed to Shui-lian. Shui-lian turned it round and round, her mouth open as she examined and counted. Looking closer, she spotted the light drawings on the surface of the lining. Ten pairs! she thought. No wonder everyone was in such a hurry. But how on earth could she do this, even if she had multiple arms, like a mythical goddess?

"Come on. Get over here. Standing there like a tree stump won't get you paid," Fang-yuan shouted over the racket. "Sit down and turn on the machine. Quick, you're wasting my time. I have my own quota to fill."

"I don't know how to operate a machine," Shui-lian said bluntly, hiding her uneasiness. "Please, teach me."

"All right, I will. But sit down first," Fang-yuan said again. "Now, turn on the switch, then put one foot on that pedal there. Press slowly but evenly. Remember, the harder you push, the faster the machine goes. It controls the speed of the needle."

Shui-lian followed Fang-yuan's directions, watching the shining needle dip and rise spasmodically. The machine seemed to have a mind of its own, she noted with alarm.

Fang-yuan continued. "While you're sewing, always keep your fingers away from the presser foot and the needle. Always keep in mind that the needle is made of steel, meant to pierce two or even more layers of leather."

Shui-lian's eyes locked on the presser foot. Beneath it, half a dozen sets of sharp teeth, pointing upward, moved back and forth hungrily as soon as she placed her foot on the pedal. She could see that the teeth were there to grab and pull the material under the presser foot while the needle plunged through it.

Fang-yuan took a piece of fabric out of her pocket and placed it on the surface of the machine in front of Shui-lian. "Use this for practice, to sew straight and curved lines. Pay attention; you won't be paid a penny until you can sew properly, so don't sit like a Buddha statue in a shrine. Start right now! You want to be a worker, don't you? So act like one." Before she turned to leave, she added, "If you need me, I'm over there, three machines down on your left."

Pan-pan leaned against her rolled-up quilt that was wedged against the metal frame of her bunk. Across from her, Shui-lian had dozed off despite the heat and chit-chat humming up and down the aisle. Pan-pan let her mind wander for a change. It had been more than four weeks since she and Shui-lian arrived at the factory and became sewing machine operators. She was thankful for her good fortune that, when she was little, her mother had taught her how to use a sewing machine. She thought about Ah-Po, hoping she remembered to take her blood pressure pills without Pan-pan there to remind her. She smiled when little Gui-yang came to mind. He would be two years old in one month. No doubt Xin-Ma would continue to spoon-feed him for fear that her precious little boy wouldn't eat enough if he was left to eat by himself.

She wondered if Lao Ma and Lao Zhang were still talking about her given her unannounced departure. They'd be disappointed for sure, or even angry—particularly Lao Zhang, who had tried the hardest to get her to change her plans. From the moment Pan-pan stepped into her house, Lao Zhang had decided to make Pan-pan's welfare her personal responsibility, embarking on a mission to send Pan-pan back to Guizhou and her family. Yet under her very nose, the girl who was only a few years older than her sons had vanished in the same manner as she had barged into their lives.

Thinking about her village and her family, Pan-pan was once again gripped with heart-rending homesickness, the same kind of sadness that had overwhelmed her when her mother died. Turning toward the wall, she wiped away her tears with the

Shui-lian remained seated, still and stiff. Her feet felt like they were made of stone or, worse, bolted to the ground. Her eyes glazed over, failing to focus on the marked lines on the fabric; her heart pounded along with the thunder created by the more than two hundred machines, angrily drumming louder and louder. All around her, their heads bent over, backs hunched, and fingers flying, the workers looked as if they too were machines. The jabbing needles, the spinning thread spools, and winding belts—all appeared aggressive and ruthless.

Shui-lian watched from her seat, seized with panic and frustration, while at the same time overwhelmed by a flood of shame and helplessness. All these women were braver and more capable than she. When she finally raised her hands to the machine, her fingers were as rigid as wooden chopsticks. She let out a slow sigh, wondering how come Jin-lin, her knowledgeable friend, had never mentioned one word about how difficult it was to be a factory worker: the intensity and racket, the lack of proper training and teaching.

Shui-lian placed her foot on the pedal and slowly pushed it down. The machine clattered. The needle rose and fell and rose again. Tentatively, she nudged the fabric under the presser foot, felt the teeth touching her fingertips before the needle punched through it as easy as a river snake swallows a rat. Maybe this isn't so bad after all, she thought, curbing her fears.

But her relief was short-lived. The machine seemed to have a mind of its own, and she spent the rest of her shift muttering and cursing as she battled her mechanical foe.

THAT NIGHT Shui-lian dreamt that she was at home on the Jialing River, sitting in the stern as the boat drifted from port to port under a vast blue sky, mountains on either side. A bamboo raft floated by on the jade-green water. Everywhere she turned to look, she was greeted with silence: the waves that hit the side of the boat, the pullers striving up high on the banks. Even the normally rackety seagulls were shushed, soundlessly flapping their wings and circling above the water. The serenity began to frighten her as she remembered that since coming onboard she hadn't seen her mother and sister, nor her brother and his new bride. "Mama, where are you?" she called out frantically, struggling to her feet. But a silent wave rolled over the stern, snatched her up, and threw her into the river. She repeatedly called her mother as she was dragged deep down into the water. Her shouts turned to bubbles before her eyes as she kicked her feet. She awoke to her own screams.

Chapter Fifteen

Summer rushed in and descended on the plain earlier than usual. The unseasonably high temperatures turned the crammed dorm into a furnace and the occupants into powder kegs. Fights erupted over the slightest annoyance and turf wars broke out daily over control of the taps and space in the washing station, for the washing period had been reduced to fifteen minutes daily because of a water shortage. The dry winter followed by a rainless spring had put a strain on the three wells that supplied fresh water for the eight hundred or so workers. People had been complaining for weeks about discovering red thread-thin worms twitching and wriggling at the bottom of their washbasins.

Mr. Tom and Mr. Tony, who lived in villas on the outskirts of Bozhou, carried their water bottles everywhere they went in the factory. Fearful of an outbreak of dysentery, they ordered the canteen staff to provide the workshops with boiled water; meanwhile, if any worker was caught drinking directly from the tap, he or she would be fined half a day's pay. But their concern lasted only until they returned to their villas each evening. Thirsty and exhausted, the nightshift workers fought over every drop of drinking water because the canteen closed after serving the midnight meal and the supply of boiled water was cut off.

corner of the bedsheet and reached under the pillow for the envelope that contained her half-written letter home. She must finish it soon and send it. It had been over a month since she had said goodbye to Ah-Po and Xin-Ma. They must be worried sick by now.

Pan-pan had begun the letter on the night after her first day of work. As soon as supper was over and she was back in the dorm, she sat down on a large empty electric cable spool that had been tucked under the bunk bed, before smoothing out a piece of filmy paper on top of her bed.

"I wish I could write as well as you," Shui-lian had commented, stretching out on her bunk across the aisle, watching Pan-pan. "If I'd known that learning to write would be useful someday, I'd have paid more attention to the teachers at the floating school, instead of blathering to Jin-lin."

"It was my mom who kept pushing me to learn, to practise, and to go to school every day," Pan-pan had replied. "But I still don't know all the words I need. I guess I'll have to use *pin-yin* to fill in the blanks." Holding the pen her mother had used when she was alive, Pan-pan looked over her shoulder at her friend. "If you want, I can write a letter for you after I finish mine." Right away Pan-pan wished she hadn't made the offer. Shui-lian had told her that her family boat had to travel from one river to another, looking for work. Even if Shui-lian could write the letter herself, she wouldn't know where to post it to. Pan-pan slowly put down her pen and carefully folded the paper. She should wait until things settled down a bit, or finish her letter when Shui-lian wasn't around.

Things could only get better from now on, she assured herself. I'm a worker now, and so is Shui-lian. When our three-month probation is over, we'll get a raise to five hundred yuan a month, more money than I would ever make if I stayed in the village, tilling earth and growing crops. In no time I'll be able to replace the money the thief snatched from my hands.

Pan-pan smiled inwardly as she once again pictured a prosperous future ahead of her, the life of the first factory worker in her family. And maybe, she thought, unconsciously squeezing her arms to her sides, I can do something about my condition, put an end to the fear and nervousness I feel each time someone around me twitches her nose. To cope with the rising temperature and lack of water and privacy, she had tried to keep awake at night until everyone was asleep. She would then reach for the tin of powder, which was tucked deep into the corner of her bed, sprinkle some onto her open palm, and apply it to her armpits, hoping that her diligence as well as the white contents would keep her safe from being exposed and ridiculed.

ACROSS THE AISLE, Shui-lian lay in bed, searching for a comfortable position. Darkness had brought little relief from the sweltering heat. On the contrary, the temperature rose inside the dorm after the door was shut and locked, leaving the sleepers to simmer in sweat, breathing stale air ripened with the funk of spoiled food, hastily washed bodies, and piles of dirty clothes under each bunk. She was exhausted beyond words, yet the aching in her neck and back from hunching over the sewing machine for twelve hours running kept sleep away. The burning in her eyes had been getting worse every day, even when they were closed. The strain of endless staring at the needle and the precision of the stitching required such a high degree of concentration that she wondered, as she had many times before, if her eyes would eventually give up blinking. The throbbing in her fingertip, wrapped in a bandage, reminded her of another miserable failure to meet her daily quota. This time the needle had punched right through the first finger of her left hand, chipping off a corner of the nail. Shui-lian had never seen so much blood in her life, hers or anyone else's. Within seconds it had soaked the white leather strips she was sewing and oozed through the lining and onto the machine top. The sight frightened her so much she didn't even feel the pain until later.

On the way to the factory clinic, Elder Sister Meng had told Shui-lian that she was lucky. The needle had punctured only the tip of her finger, not her hand, as had happened to others. One young woman from Yunnan Province, Elder Sister Meng recalled, had somehow managed to stitch her hand and the shoe upper she was working on together. "After that terrible incident, she couldn't stop shaking whenever she sat down at her machine. Yet she refused to quit," the director said, shaking her head.

"What happened to her then?"

"She was reassigned to the assembly workshop. But she wasn't there long before they let her go. This time, I heard, something went wrong in her head. It's not that she went crazy or anything. She started complaining about headaches. Then one day she fell off her stool and rolled over on the ground, wrapping her arms around her head and screaming. The doctor said her headache was caused by toxic fumes from the chemicals used for making shoes. You know what, Shui-lian?" Elder Sister Meng halted briefly. "Let's face it. Not everyone is meant to work in factories. Some people are better to stay where they are and live the way they're used to.

"Try harder, Shui-lian," Elder Sister Meng then urged her in her singsong voice. "Don't just move your fingers, make them fly. Remember, you're dealing with machines now, not dirt and seeds and night soil anymore."

"I will, Elder Sister Meng," Shui-lian promised.

SURROUNDED BY THE SNORES and breathing of her dorm mates, Shui-lian knew that no failure weighed heavier than the disappointment she felt in herself. Since she was old enough to think independently, besides her dreams of escaping a life on the water, Shui-lian had always wanted to be a worker, though she was fully aware that there would be greater chance of being eaten alive by a river carp. Even without Jin-lin's constant chatter that workers enjoyed a privileged life of ease, security, and wealth, Shui-lian desired an existence that would not expose her to the rain and wind, nor the risk of falling into the river and disappearing. The craving had been so strong and desperate it had led her to be swindled and ruined by thugs like Da-Ge. The same longing had pushed her through the gates of the Niavia Shoe Company. Now Elder Sister Meng's comments swept what fragments remained of her dreams from her head once and for all. How come Jin-lin had never mentioned that a worker's life could be so hectic and ruthless and full of danger?

The itch and irritation caused by heat rash, which had suddenly burst out one day and quickly spread over her body, were also driving her mad. Like most workers, she had a large patch of red, bumpy spots on her neck, from which white pus seeped. Earlier that night, as Pan-pan was making up her bed, her talcum powder tin had fallen to the floor, bringing a loud cheer of delight and relief in the dorm and a flash of panic to Pan-pan's face.

"Heat rash powder!" one woman exclaimed as she rushed to pick it up and read the label aloud. "Pan-pan, you're a life saver!"

Without asking permission, she unscrewed the lid, shook out a palmful of powder and dusted her neck, upper chest, and armpits before handing it to another outstretched hand. Shui-lian sat, leaning against the wall in shadow, watching the tin pass like a trophy from one person to another.

As the white powder rose into the air, her sense of resentment toward Pan-pan swelled. Here we go again, she grumbled to herself, fixing a stare of annoyance on her friend. Am I the only one who has a nose in this place, smelling her strong body odours?

The soft-spoken and good-natured Pan-pan had been popular from the beginning in comparison to Shui-lian. "They're as opposite as day and night," Shui-lian had heard one woman remark one night when she thought Shui-lian was asleep, just weeks after she and Pan-pan started working at Niavia.

"One is a hothead and quick-tempered, like a firecracker ready to explode at any time," a different voice cut in. "But she has a slow pair of hands, almost dim-witted when contrasted with her younger cousin."

"And an accident magnet," added a third. "She won't last long if she doesn't improve soon. But Pan-pan has a future here for sure."

Lying there, it was all Shui-lian could manage not to jump out of bed and light into those who dared to trash her behind her back. Pan-pan had warned her more than once that if she ever picked a fight with the dorm mates without good reason, she would be totally on her own.

But the powder's soothing effect was short-lived. In less than half an hour, the women started to complain that the heat had turned the powder into paste, clogging their pores and causing more irritation.

Serves you all right, Shui-lian said to herself, pretending to be asleep. And you too, Pan-pan. Now that the powder is gone, you have nothing left to hide your secret.

IN THE DARKNESS, Pan-pan turned and tossed. Around her, the dorm choir, as she called it, was tuning up. Although Pan-pan was accustomed to Ah-Po's snores and was familiar with the evening noises of the country, she had no idea that being awake in a roomful of sleepers could be so unsettling and, at times, frightening. Night after night, as soon as the lights were out, it seemed, the strange sound moved in, taking over and filling the corners of the tiny dorm: soft mumbles, rhythmical nose whistles, shouts, and screams. The young woman on the top bunk above her was talking rapidly to herself in her sleep. Someone else was weeping in her dreams. Yet nothing was worse than the sound of teeth grinding, so unbearable that Pan-pan often had to cover her ears, at the same time unconsciously licking her own teeth.

Across from her, Shui-lian called out in her distinctive accent. Even in her dreams, her high-pitched voice was demanding. But it was Shui-lian's cool look during the powder episode that kept playing in Pan-pan's mind. She tried to figure out Shui-lian's uncharacteristic silence and calm. Shui-lian hadn't seemed surprised when the powder tin fell onto the ground, as if she'd known Pan-pan had it all along. Yet Shui-lian had never mentioned one word to her. Most worrisome was that Shui-lian was the only one who didn't ask for the powder—everyone else, it appeared, couldn't get enough of it. The answer was as clear as it was obvious. Shui-lian knew Pan-pan's condition, and by refusing the powder, she showed her fear that the fox smell would be passed on to her. Does that mean she would refuse to be my friend as well, like the girls in the village? Pan-pan moaned, squeezing her eyes shut. Now with no more talcum powder left, her secret was going to be exposed for sure, and abandonment and taunt would be the result.

She couldn't understand how Shui-lian had found her out, for she had been so careful to maintain her nightly ritual. Occasionally she'd skip a day here and there, but she struggled to carry on despite her growing doubt about the powder's effectiveness in such extreme heat. Once the hot weather arrived, everyone in the dorm wore as little clothing as possible to keep cool. Pan-pan was the only one who wore a long-sleeved blouse. "The scholar," her dorm mates called her, taking it as a sign of formality. Obviously, Shui-lian thought differently.

I'm trapped, Pan-pan thought, before finally drifting off to sleep.

Chapter Sixteen

The physical fatigue caused by heat, lack of sleep, and long hours of intense labour was offset by good news one night when the exhausted workers were about to go to bed. Everyone was to have a day off on May 1, to commemorate International Labour Day. When the news came, cheers and laughter filled the tiny room. Shui-lian and others slapped their hands on the wooden boards in rhythm, while a couple of the women began to dance, stamping their bare feet on the dirt floor, twitching and twirling in their panties and tank tops.

But on the night of April 30, as Pan-pan and Shui-lian sat with the others in the sweltering dorm chatting about their plans for the next day, Elder Sister Meng pushed open the door. She stood there for a moment before speaking.

"I have news," she announced, raising her reedy voice above the clattering and laughing women. "Bad news."

Silence fell as all eyes turned her way.

"Mr. Tom and Mr. Tony are leaving Niavia," Elder Sister Meng said. "The new general manager is named Mr. Wu. He has called a meeting for tomorrow morning at nine sharp. Your May Day holiday is cancelled." And before Shui-lian could utter the curse that had formed on her lips, Elder Sister Meng disappeared out the door.

In the canteen the next day, the new general manager informed the assembly that he didn't want to be called Mister. "Ah-Wu" was what he preferred, he said in a thick accent. And he was a Taiwan Chinese, not a mainlander, like those in his audience.

"What is he talking about?" someone whispered behind Shui-lian. "Isn't Taiwan a part of China?"

Ah-Wu stood still on a temporary platform, waiting for the hum to die down, his tiny black eyes squinting at the roomful of workers sitting cross-legged on the cement floor. He then held up his right hand for silence as he smacked his lips, producing an awful, wet sound.

"I heard what you're saying. It's true that you and I share the same ancestor, the Yellow Emperor, but our similarity ends right there because we've been travelling on different paths for over half a century. Mine in Taiwan turned out to be a sunlit multilane freeway, and yours ..." He let his voice trail, and a sly grin appeared on his flat face. "Anyway, the result is that I am standing here as your boss, and you are my labourers."

Ah-Wu paused, enjoying the stillness, before resuming his lecture. "In some countries and cultures, revealing one's wealth is regarded as showy, even arrogant. That's not what I believe. On the contrary, I call that attitude false humility." He let out a wicked laugh, which to Shui-lian sounded like an owl's cries. "I for one don't intend to hide from you or anyone how much money I make as your general manager because as far as I'm concerned it represents my value. The truth is, what I earn in one month here is fifty percent of what all of you make, in total, in the same amount of time. Not to mention that my pay is in real money, U.S. dollars. Now," he paused again, his eyes sweeping across the audience, "let's have a bit of fun, shall we? I'm going to ask you to take a simple test, to see if any of you are up to it. You all know how much you make each month—five hundred yuan, give or take. There are eight hundred workers here, again give or take. Now, who can tell me how much money I make in a month? Whoever comes closest will be given one American dollar as a reward." He crossed his arms on his narrow chest and waited.

There had been meetings before, held by Mr. Tom and Mr. Tony with their interpreters, passing down the rules and regulations, and once or twice, announcing new orders and decrees from Elder Miss Gong, but nothing like this. Beside Pan-pan, Shui-lian stared unseeingly at the back of the person sitting in front of her. The workers tried to work out the answer to Ah-Wu's question. Some frowned intensely; a couple calculated on their open palms by using their fingertips as pens, multiplying and dividing.

Pan-pan, who was quick with numbers—something Ah-Po had always claimed with pride—had her answer ready. "About twenty-five thousand U.S. dollars a month," she said in a shaky voice.

Hundreds of eyes turned in Pan-pan's direction. "Are you sure? How did you do that so fast?" Shui-lian whispered.

"My, oh my, this is something," Ah-Wu crowed, rubbing his palms together, his roving eyes stopping on Pan-pan. "I wonder if today's your lucky day or you just made a lucky guess. Very close indeed. Now for your reward." He smirked, took a wad of money out of his pocket, peeled one note off, and handed it to a worker in the front row, who turned and passed it back to Pan-pan. "Your lucky day," Ah-Wu repeated.

Red-faced, feeling uneasy about the attention, Pan-pan wished she had the nerve to stand up and tell Ah-Wu that it had nothing to do with luck or guesswork. Keep your money, just give me due credit! she wanted to shout.

At the end of that meeting, Ah-Wu declared that no one would have a day off until the factory fulfilled its quota of one hundred thousand pairs of shoes each month, the target set by Elder Miss Gong months ago but never achieved when Mr. Tom and Mr. Tony were in charge. Up until then, the workers had gotten a free Sunday every two weeks.

"He's trying to squeeze fat from bones," Pan-pan whispered. "Even harnessed donkeys have breaks."

Everyone knew that production had been rising steadily in the past twelve months. The output had tripled to ninety thousand pairs of shoes per month, while the number of workers had merely doubled. Yet the owner wasn't satisfied.

That night, on their way to the shop to start the evening shift, Pan-pan explained to Shui-lian that it was the mention of American money that had made Ah-Wu's so-called challenge as easy as eating a bowl of rice.

"I just happened to remember from a conversation that what we're making each day is equivalent to two U.S. dollars, *give or take*," Pan-pan began, mimicking Ah-Wu's accent. "From there, it was easy. It wasn't a test at all but his way of putting us down, of saying that he's smarter than all of us, and worthier. I'd love to see if he's able to do what we do each day—sew ten pairs of shoe uppers in each shift. That's four hundred and forty pieces," Pan-pan grumbled.

Yawning and stretching in an effort to chase away their fatigue from the lack of rest and sleep, the women entered the sewing shop. Their plastic slippers dragged and clicked on the concrete floor despite the constant warnings of Elder Sister Meng that they were breaking the safety rules by wearing them. Before he left, Mr. Tom had imposed a five-yuan fine on anyone who wore slippers to work. Still, no one paid attention to this rule, particularly during the evening shift, when darkness reigned. Proper shoes cost too much, not to mention that they grew hot and uncomfortable over the long hours of sitting in one position inside the stifling workshop.

"Does anyone know how much a pair of Niavia shoes we make here cost in America?" someone asked.

"How much?"

"Too much."

"Come on, tell us if you know. Otherwise just shut up and give us a few minutes of quiet," said another.

"More than one hundred U.S. dollars, which means that what we earn in one month can buy only one shoe."

"Tell me you just made that up," Pan-pan cut in.

"I wish I had," the woman replied and walked on, leaving Pan-pan standing in the middle of an aisle.

Throughout the shift, while Pan-pan hunched over the machine amid the racket and dust, heat and sour air, her thoughts were in turmoil. The brief conversation about the price of the shoes she was making kept repeating inside her head as she stitched leather pieces onto the lining, one after another, with no end. She tried again to picture the kind of woman or man who could afford to put these white-as-chalk, soft-as-clouds shoes on their feet, then walk through mud or run through ditches. But she failed. On the other hand, knowing that no worker in the factory would ever be able to buy a single pair, even though thousands were made by their hands each day and night, was a bitter mockery. Her head began to spin as she calculated the profit Elder Miss Gong had been making since the factory opened.

Ah-wu might have more money than Shui-lian could ever comprehend, but on her first payday she felt rich, gazing at two one-hundred-yuan notes and some change after the deduction for her share of room, electricity, and water. Now I can buy my own bedding, she thought. She had never had so much money, not to mention in hundred-yuan notes. Each time she thought of Pan-pan's one U.S. dollar, she couldn't stop imagining what a thick pile of American money should have done for Ah-Wu. Yet he didn't look happy or satisfied; on the contrary, most of the time he appeared to be miserable. Shui-lian was convinced that, except for his occasional short outbursts of laughter, which sounded more sad than merry, it would take a chisel to crack a smile on Ah-Wu's mournful face. The corners of his tiny eyes remained curved downward, as did his lips, even when he was shouting at people. And he was all skin and bones, with a flat behind and protruding joints, like a walking skeleton. Surely Ah-Wu was able to eat meat every day and any other kind of food money could buy, Shui-lian thought, yet he looked like he was starving.

"What's he doing with his money?" she asked Pan-pan one day. "Paving roads all over Taiwan?"

The workers soon discovered Ah-Wu's other obsession, besides putting down everyone in the factory, including his drones: his love of liquor—not beer or the cheap wine the male workers treated themselves to once in a while inside their dorms. Ah-Wu was after the real, hard stuff. It was said his favourite was the famous *Mao-tai,* a strong spirit made from rice and water from a special spring in Guizhou. Each bottle cost more than a worker's monthly wage. Like a wild cat that sleeps by day and hunts by night, Ah-Wu spent his days in his stylish villa and came to the factory just before dark, where he drank by himself in his office until the break of dawn.

Within a week after Ah-Wu took the position, he began a thorough housecleaning, laying off half the administrators and office clerks, including Mr. Yao and his deputies, and replacing them with a group of eight men he had brought with him. All eight came from Fujian, a southern province of China, from the village where Ah-Wu's father had lived until he left for Taiwan as a young soldier in the Nationalist Army on the eve of the Communist takeover. During the day, while Ah-Wu was nursing his intoxicated body in his villa, his Demons, as they were called behind their backs, terrorized the factory.

The Demons and their boss were as different as day and night. While Ah-Wu favoured oversized shirts with loud, busy prints and skinny-legged *niu-zai-ku*—cowboy pants—the Demons dressed in black *gong-fu*–style jackets with mandarin collars and baggy pants. Even their hair styles contrasted with

Ah-Wu's. The Demons had long, greasy hair, parted in the middle and hanging down to their shoulders. Ah-Wu kept his short, and puffy on the top. Whereas he was clean shaven, his henchmen sported stubble that reminded Pan-pan of rice stalks cut by inexperienced hands.

The Demons called one another *xiong-di*—brother—and their rank was set by Ah-Wu in accordance with their degree of blood relation to his family. Demon Number One, a stringy man with a long, sad face, was Ah-Wu's first cousin on his father's side, while Demon Two was a relative from his mother's. And Demon Eight, a short, solid man who was also the youngest of the bunch, was the only son of a brother of Ah-Wu's second cousin's husband. For Pan-pan, it brought to mind a verse she learned to recite as a child: When someone in the family rose to the position of a mandarin in the imperial court, even the household's dogs and chickens were distinguished.

To Pan-pan, even without their ferocious looks, the Demons resembled the statues of villains that stood outside the newly restored temple on the mountaintops near her village. Pan-pan wondered if Ah-Wu had held an "ugliest man" pageant in his father's village and retained the top eight finalists.

The Demons swaggered around the compound, bullying and harassing the workers at will, in particular the women. It didn't take them long to learn that it was the Demons' hands that were the greatest threat. When the Demons were not idle or standing with their arms folded across their chests, they wandered up and down between the rows of machines, scrutinizing the sewing women, poised to slap the back of their heads or the sides of their faces on the slightest pretext. The only thing missing from the picture was long whips, Pan-pan thought bitterly, recalling an old poster Ah-Po had hung on the wall of their bedroom for many years until time and dust devoured it. It depicted a fierce-looking man, supposedly a pre-liberation landlord, holding a whip over a kneeling peasant. Ah-Po had insisted the discoloured picture was there to remind her, and Pan-pan, of the suffering of the poor farmers before the Communist Party liberated China. What would Ah-Po say now if she were here? A Demon looming behind me, ready to strike.

The Demons' tyranny and constant presence hit Shui-lian particularly hard. Their aggression and brutality brought back memories she was trying to forget, and gave her new nightmares. Although she had never seen the faces of her attackers on that horrible night months ago, any whiff of the Demons' smell—a noxious brew of sweat, cigarettes, and liquor—was enough to terrify her, causing her to flinch at the sewing machine and miss or skip stitches. More than once she froze and forgot to move her foot off the pedal and her fingers away from the presser foot, watching helplessly as the running needle wrecked the leather piece and hurt her hands. She paid a fine for the damage and was given a severe warning.

It was the face of Demon Six that terrified her the most. Sometimes at night she was too afraid to close her eyes in the dark. Shui-lian didn't know when Demon Six, a stocky, neckless man in his late thirties, had first taken a special interest in her.

One morning, Shui-lian was hurrying back to her machine from the washroom. She quickened her steps, worried that she might have overstayed her allotted time. According to the new rules, taking too long in the toilet would not just bring her a penalty but affect other workers as well. In addition to the old rule that gave every worker a fifteen-minute washroom break, twice in each shift, Ah-Wu's new regulation had gone farther, turning the toilet breaks into a relay game. Now no one was allowed to leave until the person before them had returned. Ah-Wu called it a "system of responsibility."

One minute Shui-lian was cursing Ah-Wu under her breath as a mean and cruel son of a dog, the next, she saw a shadow move sideway toward her, like a creeping crab, and stop, blocking her path. She crashed headfirst into a barrel-like chest. Demon Six's face almost touched hers, and his smile was more like a grimace. He placed a meaty hand on one of Shui-lian's shoulders.

"My little country sister," he said in a lustful tone. "How about having some fun with me after your shift?"

"Take your hand off me, Boss," Shui-lian replied, twisting out of his grasp. Head low, staring at the tips of her shoes, she stood, waiting for Demon Six to move out of her way. Her arms hung at her sides, her hands closed in fists to conceal her tremors.

"I like that. Calling me your boss," said Demon Six, reaching to touch her chin. When Shui-lian attempted to step back, Demon Six took hold of her. Trapping her in his short arms, he ground his pelvis against hers.

"Oh, my Lord," he moaned playfully, his eyes half closed. "Fresh tits. No bra. What a treat! You're quite a she-devil, aren't you? What a waste, though, hidden away in these shapeless rags. I'll dress you up nicely."

"Let go of me, you pig!" Shui-lian hissed, struggling to block the hand trying to get inside her shirt. Bending her head, she sank her teeth into his shoulder.

"Ouch!" Demon Six cried out, releasing her and jumping backwards. "Little bitch! I'm going to pull out all your teeth, one at a time, see if you dare open your mouth again!"

He grabbed a fistful of Shui-lian's hair in one hand and cocked his fist, ready to punch her face. From the corner of his eye, he caught sight of two male workers standing nearby, staring wordlessly. He turned and nodded at them meaningfully before letting go of Shui-lian.

Shui-lian dashed back to the shop and took her place. Panting, her heart thumping, she willed herself to calm down. Her skin crawled, her stomach heaved.

That night, Shui-lian stayed awake long after curfew. When she was sure everyone was sound asleep, she sat up quietly and, groping in the dark, reached under her pillow for a handful of wide cloth strips she had ripped from a worn blouse. She pulled off her old T-shirt. Using her palm to smooth the cotton strips, one at a time, she began to wrap her chest, round and round, tighter with each turn, to flatten her breasts. Her eyes stung with tears as she tried to shut out the scene when Demon Six attacked her, observed by two strange men. How she wished her mother were there to comfort and protect her. On second thought, she was relieved her mother knew nothing about this or the other things she had suffered since leaving home two months ago—though it felt more like two years. After she finished wrapping herself, Shui-lian lay back down. Turning from side to side, she found a position that seemed to ease the tightness enfolding her chest. She closed her eyes against the pain, dreading the next day but glad that, for a few hours at least, the lock on the door would protect her.

Chapter Seventeen

Pan-pan sensed that something more than the latest sewing injury was taking a heavy toll on Shui-lian. She seemed to have aged overnight. Her usually glowing face was doughy and pale, as if the bleeding from her wound had drained her dry. Her pretty eyes, which often sparkled like ripples in a river even when they were tired, had turned empty and dull. They were puffy and swollen with sadness. Even her movement was different: When she walked, she held her upper body rigid and stiff like a board. Gone were her bouncy and graceful steps. And she avoided eye contact with everyone throughout the morning washing and breakfast, Pan-pan included, like they were strangers.

Pan-pan wished Shui-lian would confide in her and tell her what was bothering her. She was crushed by the alienation growing between them and missed the laughter they had shared since the day they met. Their fun had come easily—loud and bubbling—sometimes annoying their dorm mates. Twice she was about to ask Shui-lian what was troubling her; twice she stopped at the last minute after reminding herself that Shui-lian sometimes was moody, or touchy, as indeed others had commented behind Shui-lian's back. It scared Pan-pan when she thought that Shui-lian might have decided to abandon her, just like some girls in her village had. Or is it Shui-lian's resentment, even jealousy, that is tearing us apart? she wondered. But it's not my fault that I'm less intimidated by the sewing machine than she is, that I'm so far accident-free and making steady progress at work.

Pan-pan knew she was lucky because she wasn't a complete stranger to a sewing machine. Her mother had owned one, a wedding present from Ah-Po and Auntie Cai-fei. Mom had loved to make her own clothes and, later, most of Pan-pan's. She had also taught Pan-pan how to operate her machine, which was not much different from the ones in the workshop. It had a wide square treadle made of cast iron, a small hand wheel, and a large foot wheel connected by a leather belt rather than a motor, as in the factory. But the only damage Mom's machine could cause was breaking a needle when the wheels spun backwards, which had never resulted in bleeding and injuries like those Shui-lian and other workers had suffered. It's true that Mom's machine was much slower, but still ... Pan-pan was lost in her train of thought. But what was the hurry anyway, and what was the frantic need for such a great number of shoes? Hundreds of thousands, even millions of pairs from one factory alone.

Pan-pan had asked a few times to be moved closer to Shui-lian in the workshop, so that she could be close to her friend. But her requests had been denied. Her machine was so far away from Shui-lian's it might as well have been in a different building. A few times, particularly after the accidents, if the Demons were not watching, she would quietly slip by Shui-lian on her way to her toilet or meal breaks and drop a number of her own finished pieces into her bin, so that Shui-lian wouldn't be too far off her daily quota. Each time Shui-lian averted her eyes and pretended she didn't see, nor did she mention as much as one word about them.

At the shop entrance, Pan-pan stole a last look at Shui-lian before heading to the opposite corner to start another shift of endless sewing. She was hurt by Shui-lian's silence. At the same time she realized that she herself wasn't being totally open and honest with her friend. She wondered what Ah-Po or her father, or even Xin-Ma, would have done in her situation. And what they would have said if they knew what was going on behind the tall and forbidding wall of Niavia.

THROUGHOUT THE DAY, Shui-lian flinched each time she caught black pants legs moving toward her. She skipped her midday toilet break and trailed closely behind Pan-pan and other workers at meal times. It was the longest day she had ever spent. When the quitting bell finally rang, she could barely stand up, her legs like soft cotton from tension and exhaustion. The sweat-soaked strips around her chest were suffocating her, shortening her breath. She felt nauseated and couldn't wait to get back to the dorm, lie down, and close her burning eyes.

Leaving the sewing shop, she was stopped by Demon Five, or "Flesh Hammer" as he proudly called himself because he was always ready to punch anyone who dared to talk back to him. He had once slugged a male worker so hard he bruised all four knuckles on his right hand. Most female workers shied away from him as soon as they saw his shadow. But today there was nowhere for Shui-lian to hide or retreat when Demon Four stepped behind her, blocking that path.

"You," Demon Five grunted, pointing his finger. "Office."

"Why me?" Shui-lian asked lamely.

Pan-pan stopped. A few departing workers also held back.

"Don't ask questions!" Demon Five screamed, stepping closer, glaring down at Shui-lian. "I don't haggle with worthless women like you. Office!"

"I'll come with you," said Pan-pan, but she was confronted by a thick arm that cut in between her and Shui-lian.

"No, I'll go. I'll be okay," Shui-lian said in a hushed voice. Without looking at Demon Five, she turned and headed toward the office.

"Shui-lian, wait!" Pan-pan called after her, but her friend walked on and disappeared behind the building.

Inside the office, sitting behind the desk that used to be Mr. Yao's, Demon Three, the director of People's Affairs, was on the phone, nodding and repeating, "*Shi, shi, shi*—yes, yes, yes." Demon Six stood behind him, picking his nose. He sneered at Shui-lian as soon as she came in. Shui-lian looked away, avoiding his stare, and fixed her eyes on the bare, whitewashed wall. She was nervous but not as frightened as she thought she would be, and that surprised her. It's still light outside, and Pan-pan as well as a roomful of workers know where I am. If worse comes to worst, she said to herself, biting her lip, this time I'll fight until my last breath.

The overhead fan revolved round and round, squeaking and wobbling. Finally the director put down the phone. Stone-faced, he told Shui-lian to step closer to him and began to speak calmly. He didn't mention one word of what had happened between her and Demon Six. Instead, he told Shui-lian that because of her poor performance in the sewing shop, she was being transferred to the Cutting Department, starting with the next shift.

"I warn you," he said, his voice firm, "if you fail again, you'll only have yourself and your dirt-filled head to blame."

Shui-lian stood still, so dumbfounded the insult failed to register. She had heard about transfers between workshops, but it usually happened for a reason. Despite her latest accident, Shui-lian's sewing skill had been steadily improving. Even Elder Sister Meng had said so, praising Shui-lian for finally getting over her "machine fear." So why the transfer now? Most of all, why the cutting shop, a place filled with more challenging machinery and employing largely male workers?

In the past two months, mostly through gossip in the dorm, Shui-lian had learned a bit more about the three other shops. The most sought-after one was General Assembly, where the shoes were put together. Equipped with three production lines and used equipment shipped from a factory in Taiwan, it was the least crowded. Except for the toxic fumes from glue and other chemicals, it was considered relatively quiet, clean, and safe. Despite the tragedy that happened to the girl from Yunnan, still no one considered the strong smells hazardous. It was no secret that most of the employees there were members of managers' immediate families, other relatives, and friends.

The Insole Making Department was the dirtiest. Shui-lian had heard that the air was so thick with dust that the workers bumped into one another when they moved around, or banged into the machines and other equipment. Looming clouds of black and white powder from various chemical compounds hung heavily day and night inside the poorly ventilated workshop.

The most dangerous department was Cutting, also known as the "amputation shop." It was outfitted with vertical and horizontal shears and other machines, among them punching cutters, which had proved as treacherous as they were unreliable. Like madmen with unpredictable fits, time and again they would malfunction, the cutter thrusting downward without any warning and causing grave injuries, from crushed hands and fingers to, once, a severed forearm.

Shui-lian didn't know how long she remained frozen, gazing at a fixed point on the floor. A slap on the desktop brought her back from her thoughts.

"Now, get out," Demon Three ordered. "I don't want to see you back here again."

As Shui-lian turned to leave, she caught sight of Demon Six making a slashing gesture across his neck before he threw his head back and burst out laughing.

On the way to the dorm, Shui-lian held back her tears. It was plain that the transfer was an act of pure vindictiveness, punishing her for spurning Demon Six. She thought about the evil of putting someone like her, who had just got over the fear of a sewing machine, into a room full of sharp and dangerous equipment. How could people like the Demons, Da-Ge, and the men who had violated her be so cruel? All were older than she was, and hateful toward her.

Before she reached the dorm, she realized that leaving Pan-pan and the other young women with whom she had been working and sharing the same living quarters scared her almost as much as the monstrous machines waiting for her. In over two months, she'd grown to like most of the women in the dorm—even Fang-yuan, who in the past couple of days had dropped a few finished shoe uppers into her bin when she thought Shui-lian wasn't looking.

Pushing open the dorm door she wondered, who will help me now?

Chapter Eighteen

In the dim light, Pan-pan helped Shui-lian pack her pitiful belongings and quietly added a couple of new washcloths and an undershirt to the bundle. She insisted on going with Shui-lian to her new dorm, two buildings away. Earlier, Pan-pan had cried with fury when Shui-lian told of her encounter with Demon Six the day before. Stamping her feet in anger—an action Shui-lian had never seen from her friend—Pan-pan cursed the Demons loudly. She even had gone to Elder Sister Meng, begging her to intercede, to keep Shui-lian in the sewing shop. Sending her to the cutting shop was like dropping a lamb into a tiger's den, she argued. No, Elder Sister Meng had said, it was more like killing a chicken to scare the monkeys. But there was nothing she could do.

On the way to her new dorm, Shui-lian, trying her hardest not to cry, reassured her friend, who kept wiping her eyes on the shoulder of her T-shirt.

"Don't cry, Pan-pan. We're still in the same compound, so we can still see each other. And don't worry about me; I'll be fine."

THE END OF JUNE brought another stifling heat wave rolling across the plain. At midday even the cicadas stopped their high-pitched calls. It wasn't long after Shui-lian began her new job in the cutting room that she felt a persistent tingling and aching in her throat. One night before she went to bed she vomited repeatedly, and hours later her coughing was so violent it woke everyone in the dorm. She was running a fever. But when dawn came, Shui-lian struggled to get up and go to work. She couldn't afford a sick day. Only one week remained before the end of her three-month probation. And then she would get full pay, plus the twenty percent of her wages that the company held back during the probation period. After deductions for room and board, there wasn't much to show for eleven weeks of hard labour. Nor did she want to spend money on pills or medicine. One more week left, she kept reminding herself as she walked unsteadily along the footpath. She would crawl to the shop if she had to.

In the days that followed, Shui-lian's cough got worse. Each hacking fit seemed to scour her guts and shake her tiny frame. Stable hands were an essential requirement for operating the punching cutter, under which she pushed stacks of leather or fabric to be precisely sheared by the bright, heavy blades according to the pattern—sharp turns and rigid tips and curves. Time and again, fits of coughing forced her to turn away from the machine, often bending over double and gasping for air. Even when she finally dragged herself back to the dorm at the end of her shift and was able to lie down, the back and chest pains gave her no rest.

One night during her toilet break she spotted blood in her saliva when she coughed and spat into the sink. Even though she knew very little about the significance of spitting blood, it worried her. There were only five days to go before her probation ended. She decided to say nothing, fearing that the Demons would use any excuse to punish her more. Since the transfer she hadn't seen much of them—they stayed away from the cutting shop, probably because most of the workers there were males.

She lifted the corner of her T-shirt to wipe her mouth dry before she stepped out of the washroom. The heat that had been simmering the brick walls of the compound during the day lingered. Shui-lian paused briefly on the path. She closed her eyes, took a deep breath, savouring a moment of stillness before returning to the dust, fumes, and shattering noise. The position of the quarter moon in the sky told her it must be near midnight. The workers' living quarters were cast in dark shadow. Crickets filled the silence with their chirping. On the other side of the wall, in the rice paddies, frogs croaked in one unbroken chorus. Their monotonous drone reminded her of the night she had been raped nearly three months ago.

Back in the workshop, the air seemed even more suffocating and rancid from sweaty and unwashed bodies, flying powder, and other chemical compounds. Nausea overcame Shui-lian. After pausing for another coughing spell, she struggled to get to her table. Two stacks of white linings were waiting to be sliced, the pattern clearly marked on the top sheet in black dotted lines. Shui-lian leaned against the edge of the punching cutter table, composing herself before she flipped on the switch. She bent her head down, leaning to one side so she could have a better view of the pattern. Just as she began to feed the material under the hovering blade, another coughing fit wracked her body. Thick phlegm rose to her throat, gagging her. She clapped her right hand over her mouth, but it was too late. A streak of bloody spit smeared the top sheet of the linings, obliterating some of the black tracings. Shui-lian panicked. With one hand at her mouth, she frantically wiped at the bloodstain. The punching cutter slammed down. Then came the searing pain, like an electric shock that shook her whole body. It was the last thing she remembered before she passed out.

SHUI-LIAN WOKE to the stifling midday heat, and within minutes she felt that she would skin herself alive if it would ease the maddening itching all over her body. For over a week now an ugly red rash had covered her from shoulder blades to waist. She stirred and tried to turn onto her side but failed. Her entire body seemed immobile, as if nailed to the bed. She opened her eyes and saw the blurred outline of a white object suspended above her chest. Squinting to focus, she realized it was her left arm, attached to the bunk above her by a strip of cloth. She pulled, trying to set it free, then screamed in pain.

"What's happened to me?" she cried out, but her shouts came out a murmur. She lifted her head and saw that the bunks across the aisle were empty. Where is everyone? she wondered. They should all be sleeping. Confused, she turned her head to the wall. Her eyes came to rest on the tin of heat rash powder next to the pillow. She was in Pan-pan's bed.

At that moment, the door opened. Pan-pan backed into the dorm, holding a washbasin. She turned around and smiled, put the basin filled with water on the floor, and sat down on the edge of the bunk.

"Why am I in your bed?" Shui-lian asked feebly. "What's wrong with my hand? I can't move it."

"You don't remember? You had an accident, Shui-lian. I brought you here so you'd have a better rest. It's quieter and cooler, since everyone else is away working. Talking about cooler, I have some clean, cold water here. Let me give you a sponge bath. You'll feel better."

"No, not yet. Tell me what's happened." Before she could continue, Shui-lian was seized by a fierce bout of coughing. The pain that rose into her face made Pan-pan burst into tears.

"I'm so sorry, Shui-lian," Pan-pan broke down. "It's all my fault. I shouldn't have listened to Lao Zhou. If I hadn't urged you to take the job, this would never have happened."

"What are you talking about?" Shui-lian demanded, drying her mouth with the back of her hand. Suddenly she remembered the blood in her saliva and the stain on the shoe lining. She would have to pay a heavier fine this time. "Don't worry, Pan-pan. I'm all right."

"No, you're not!" Pan-pan wailed. "Part of your thumb is gone."

"My thumb?" Shui-lian whispered. "What about my thumb? What do you mean it's gone?"

"You sheared it off last night on the cutting machine!" Pan-pan lowered her head and covered her face with her hands.

Shui-lian stared at the bare bunk above her. She made no reply, nor did she hear Pan-pan's sobs.

Chapter Nineteen

Two days later, when Pan-pan hurried along the path to the dorm on her toilet break, she was stopped by Demon Six. "Ah-Wu wants you in his office. Right now," he commanded.

"Can it wait?" Pan-pan pleaded. "I have to see if Shui-lian needs anything."

"No, it can't!" he shouted, eyes glaring. "How dare you tell Ah-Wu to wait! Especially over that trashy Guizhou drab! I thought you were the smart one."

What does Ah-Wu want? Pan-pan wondered.

The day before, Pan-pan had rushed to see Demon Three after she finished work. Hot and sweaty, hungry and thirsty, she knocked cautiously on his door. She had with her the severed piece of Shui-lian's thumb, wrapped in a scrap of shoe lining. A worker in the shop had found it and cleaned it the best way he could. He also told Pan-pan that for some time now many hospitals in China had succeeded in attaching severed limbs and fingers, if it was done in time. Pan-pan wanted one of the factory vehicles to take Shui-lian to the hospital in Bozhou to see a real doctor, rather than the woman who split her working hours between the canteen and the clinic. All that woman had done was change the blood-soaked dressing, count out pills, and punch a needle into Shui-lian's behind when the pain became too excruciating.

"She was injured on her shift, Director, and she's in awful pain. Please help her," Pan-pan had begged.

The director had sent her away, saying that he had to report to Ah-Wu.

Now, as Pan-pan followed Demon Six, her heart pounded in her throat. She tried to figure out the significance of Ah-Wu breaking his routine by showing his face in the factory when the sky was lit by the sun, not the moon or stars. Her legs weakened when she saw the windows of Ah-Wu's office, and she found herself awash with fear as the door was opened.

Ah-Wu was sitting with his sandalled feet up on a large desk. His eyes were hidden behind wraparound sunglasses. When Pan-pan sidled in and stood by the door, which was closed behind her, he wiggled his first finger, motioning her closer, until Pan-pan could see her face in his mirror-like lenses.

The office was cool and damp, a sharp contrast to the sparkling heat outside. Beside her, a motor hummed softly, a magic machine everyone had been talking about that produced cool air and heavenly comfort. The director stood behind Ah-Wu, his hands behind his back, his eyes avoiding contact with Pan-pan. Demon Six resumed his rigid position on Ah-Wu's left, his arms folded on his chest.

"Well, well, well." Ah-Wu broke the silence, swinging his legs down. He stood, leaning forward against the edge of the desk, the dark lenses aimed directly at Pan-pan. "A mathematician from …" He paused, turning his head toward the director.

"From Guizhou, Ah-Wu. The mountain people."

"Right. The mountains, which means caves, stones, and

rocks—and, surprisingly, a woman who can count." He canted his head back and burst out laughing. "I hope you haven't rushed out and spent the dollar I gave you. It's your lucky star, and you'll need it *today.*"

He yelled the last word, slapping his hand on the desk. Startled, Pan-pan took a step backwards.

"This is a factory, you country bumpkin, not a rest house. Workers getting injured is as normal as eating three meals a day," Ah-Wu ranted. "It's her own fault—her clumsiness and stupidity that cut off her thumb. But you really are something, aren't you? How dare you come here and tell us what to do? You know where the hospital is! No one is stopping you!" By now he was yelling so hard, white foam oozed from the corners of his mouth.

"But Ah-Wu," Pan-pan mustered in a trembling voice. "The hospital is too far. And she's lost so much blood. She's very weak. Besides, she can't afford the treatment, unless the factory can help her out, and—"

"—and nothing. Period." Ah-Wu cut her off, removing his dark shades and revealing bulging eyes that were puffy and criss-crossed with thin red lines. "Listen really carefully, cave woman. I am running a factory, not a charity. I'll say it one last time. The accident is all her fault. We're not paying one penny toward her medical bill."

He stopped, put his glasses back on, and chuckled. Behind him, the director scratched his head, baffled by the sudden change of mood. Even Demon Six looked bewildered, his face twitching as though he couldn't decide whether to join the laughter or keep a straight face.

"Too bad China no longer has the universal medical care the government used to brag about to the rest of the world," Ah-Wu continued, "but Canada, a country of capitalism, has it. No wonder that bloody country is called 'Everyone Takes.'" He laughed when he caught the dumbfounded look of the director.

Pan-pan raised her eyes. She knew what Ah-Wu was implying. When she was little she had heard both at home and in school the stories of Doctor Bethune, a Canadian who helped the Chinese revolution. She also knew Canada in Chinese was *Jia-na-da,* composed of three Chinese characters. With the last word moved to be the first—*da-jia-na*—it meant, "everyone takes."

Pan-pan refused to give up. "But—" she began.

"No buts," Ah-Wu snapped. He walked around the desk toward Pan-pan, who leapt backwards. Clenching her fists to stop them from trembling, she turned to leave.

"Not so fast," Ah-Wu called out, picking up a folder from the desk. "I trust this matter is solved," he said, lowering his voice dramatically. "And if I were you, I wouldn't utter one more word or blab about the incident to anyone, in particular outside the compound. There are people out there and around the world who love to criticize factories like ours. The truth is, no one tied you up and dragged you here, did they? Not to mention," he paused, flipping open the folder and pulling out a sheet of paper, "that it turns out you're the ones who have been telling us lies."

"What do you mean?"

"What I mean is this: Is it true you and Chen Shui-lian are cousins as it states here? And is it true that you're both from Guizhou Province?"

"All right, we're not cousins. But what does it matter? What's the difference whether Shui-lian is from Guizhou or not? She works as hard as any other worker, and—"

"The difference is that she's an illegal," Ah-Wu cut Pan-pan off, a vein bulging on the side of his skinny neck as his anger built up once again. "This Zhou person who filled in this form used someone else's name and national identification number to register your so-called cousin. Now you tell me, smart mouth, how in hell this Shui-lian woman could be injured in this factory if she's never worked here!"

"You, you ..." Pan-pan was so stunned by his sly logic that she failed to form a sentence. Tongue-tied, she wished she was like the people she had seen on TV, able to stay calm when confronted with crises. She wished she could do as they did: speak eloquently, use big words to argue and reason with thugs like Ah-Wu, tell him that she, as well as every other worker in the factory, knew that most of the equipment was unsafe, outdated, even obsolete, not brand new as it said on the government papers to fool the officials. She also wanted to tell him that the owner was greedy and her factory failed to provide even the basic training for the workers, that Shui-lian's transfer to the cutting shop was an act of vengeance, and the cause of her sickness and the accidents.

"Get out of here!" Ah-Wu yelled, flapping his hand as though chasing away a bug. "Go and tell your so-called cousin to pack up her bedroll. I want her out of the compound before dark or I'll throw her out myself."

When she opened the door to leave, Pan-pan heard Demon

Six snarl at her from behind. "Get back to work. Your toilet break is over."

PAN-PAN DRIED HER EYES and took a deep breath before she entered the workshop. She sat down quietly in front of her machine and turned on the switch with a shaking hand. How had they found out about Shui-lian? Pan-pan sensed that Ah-Wu as well as the director had known for some time. The fact that they had said or done nothing about it meant they couldn't have cared less whether she and Shui-lian were cousins or where Shui-lian was from as long as a young and healthy woman was hired. Ah-Wu himself had said on more than one occasion that it didn't matter to him who worked in his factory so long as the person was "in good health and not too stupid." Once he had even commented that nowadays in mainland China it was much easier to find a worker than a purebred dog. But now that Shui-lian was no longer useful to the factory and to the owner, her false identity was brought up and used against her. Pan-pan thought about all the misery and injustice Shui-lian had gone through to fulfill her dreams. Even though Pan-pan was the one who had gone to see the director, she was allowed to stay. The reason was as clear as it was simple: Pan-pan was still useful and would continue to make a profit for Ah-Wu and Elder Miss Gong. Two days short of the end of her three-month probation, Pan-pan had not just become a skilful sewing machine operator, she had outperformed many of her co-workers who had been in the factory much longer, with hardly any returns for defective work. Ah-Wu and the director knew that, too.

Thinking of her friend, Pan-pan moved her foot off the pedal and turned off her machine, leaving a half-stitched shoe-upper flattened under the presser foot. She reached down to pick up her food tin and water bowl, then stood up, brushing the dust off the front of her shirt. Looking at no one and remaining silent, she let her timecard drop to the floor and walked straight toward the entrance. Angry shouts rose from one of the Demons, ordering her back to work. Pan-pan heard him but kept walking, past the columns of noisy machines, in between the black bins. A woman on her left paused at her sewing, watching Pan-pan approach and then pass by her. More machines slowed down, a few stopped, more eyes rose to gaze at her. She felt them on her back as she continued out the door and out of their sight.

Chapter Twenty

"I can't let you do this, Pan-pan," Shui-lian said, watching Pan-pan gathering her belongings. "I don't want to be your burden anymore." Shui-lian lay on her back, listening to Pan-pan's account of her meeting with Ah-Wu. Her left arm was now slung across her chest, suspended on a leather belt looped around her neck, her bandaged thumb, a bloodstained lump. Every bit of her exposed skin was covered by a bumpy heat rash, red and angry, as though ready to explode.

"Stop talking nonsense, Shui-lian. You're not a burden. My mind is made up. We came here together and we're leaving together."

"Please, I beg you. I'll be fine. You have a future here."

One minute Shui-lian was talking, the next she was all tears, barely able to get the words out. "I'm sorry, Pan-pan." Her body shook so violently, the words left her mouth syllable by syllable.

Pan-pan stopped folding an undershirt. "What are you talking about? I should ask for your forgiveness. I'm the one who got us into this mess—slaving every day to make people like Ah-Wu rich."

"No, no." Shui-lian squeezed her eyes shut. "Pan-pan, I don't deserve your friendship and your sacrifice. I was jealous and resented you. And … and I lied to you. I didn't just run away from my abductors as I told you. I was gang-raped. So were the others I was with. And then the police came and arrested us for prostitution. I was too ashamed to tell you the truth, afraid that you would look down on me and refuse to be my friend. Now you're leaving the factory because of me. Pan-pan, how can I accept this? I'm no good to you or anyone else."

Pan-pan felt like she had been kicked in the stomach. She sat down on the edge of the bunk beside Shui-lian, numb and nauseated. She couldn't begin to imagine what Shui-lian must have suffered.

Pan-pan sat with Shui-lian for a long time, thinking. "Listen to me, Shui-lian," she said, breaking the silence. "There is nothing for me to forgive. I haven't been honest with you, either. My mother didn't die in a fall from a narrow track on a mountain. What killed her was a botched operation that she hoped would cure her fox smell. Mom thought it an unspeakably shameful social handicap. People looked down on her as if it were a disgraceful disease. And," Pan-pan paused briefly, shifting her eyes away, "I've inherited it from her. Probably you've known all along."

"Well …" Shui-lian hesitated, but Pan-pan kept on.

"Because of it, my friends and people in the village shied away from me. My Ah-Po and Xin-Ma were constantly afraid I might pass it to them and to my little brother." Reaching for the powder tin, Pan-pan continued. "And this is supposed to help me, to be my disguise and my shield. It seemed to work. When I met you I promised myself that I wasn't going to tell you about my condition. That night when you were the only one who didn't ask for the powder, I sensed that you knew, and I thought you would despise me and abandon me like everyone else. But you didn't. Shui-lian, you have no idea how relieved and grateful I was."

Pan-pan silently turned the tin round and round in her hand. "The others claimed that I had some kind of foresight when they found the powder, showering me with praise. The truth was, after the powder was gone and I couldn't find any more in the market, I just stopped worrying, because I realized everyone here smells from sweating and lack of clean water. And everywhere stinks, inside the shop and outside the compound, from the dorm to the toilets, even the washing area, and even the ditch that circles the factory's outside wall. Earlier Ah-Wu mentioned something about people around the world having all kinds of names for factories like ours. One of them is sweatshop. Well, they sure know what they're talking about. The sweat we pump out every day and night could have filled a pond by now!"

"Yes, I know. But fox smell? That's the worst gibberish I've ever heard in my life. I bet whoever came up with that exaggerated term has never laid eyes on a real fox," Shui-lian said, drying her eyes with the back of her good hand. "But I'm sorry for your mom and what you had to put up with. I wish I had known. Lao Zhou was right, calling us suffering sisters, wasn't he?" She looked up at Pan-pan. "But what are we going to do? I don't want to go home, not like this."

"I have an idea." Pan-pan spoke again. "I think we should go to Beijing. First, it's not as hot there. Your heat rash will go away. Second, we can look for Sun Ming. You remember her. Ah-Po said she was a nice girl. Of course, that was thirty years ago. But I'd like to find her. Maybe she can help us find a better job. Not making shoes, for sure, and no more dealing with Ah-Wu and his demons. After all, it's the capital city! There must be better jobs. What do you think?"

Shui-lian blinked, licking her parched lips. She opened her mouth to speak but changed her mind. She was afraid she might not have enough money to get to Beijing.

"Don't worry," Pan-pan said, as if reading her friend's mind. "I've saved enough for both of us."

"All right. Let's do it. I promise to pay you back the train fare," said Shui-lian, a weak smile appearing on her face, the first since the accident. With some effort, she swung her legs over the edge of the bed. "Let's pack up and get out of this place."

SHORTLY AFTER the shift ended, Fang-yuan rushed into the dorm, hot and sweaty, a white ring left by perspiration around her shirt collar. Most of the other women had already flopped onto their bunks and sat fanning themselves as they chatted.

Fang-yuan stood before Pan-pan, hands on hips. "Is it true that you were both fired?" she asked.

"No," Pan-pan replied calmly. "We quit."

The bamboo fans ceased flapping and the conversations died. All eyes fixed upon Pan-pan.

"You what?" Fang-yuan exclaimed, blinking in disbelief. "Tell me you're joking."

"She's not," Shui-lian put in. "I was fired, she's quitting."

"What happened?" another woman asked from the end of the room as the fans resumed their rhythms. "What did Ah-Wu have to say about that?"

Pan-pan repeated what she had told Shui-lian, but left out the part about her and Shui-lian not being cousins.

"Animals," a third woman spat. "How could anyone be so heartless? Throwing an injured girl out on the street. How can they get away with it? It's a pity labour unions no longer speak for the workers of this country. What we need is—"

"Maybe we can all go to talk to Ah-Wu," Fang-yuan interrupted. "He should realize you two are good workers."

"It's kind of you, Fang-yuan," said Pan-pan with emotion. "But Ah-Wu has made up his mind. And so have we." She paused for a second, shifting her eyes to Shui-lian, who was trying to zip up her bag with her good hand. "And we, or rather I, haven't been totally honest with you. We told you on our first day here that we were cousins."

Fang-yuan smiled. "I remember. And I got mad at you."

"Well, we aren't related. She's from Sichuan, and I'm from Guizhou. The recruiter advised us not to say she was Sichuanese. But it turns out Ah-Wu knew the truth all along."

Elder Sister Meng, who had dropped by the dorm to say goodbye, asked, "And he used this against you?"

Pan-pan nodded. "You could say that."

"But, Pan-pan, you're giving up your job because someone who is not even related to you got fired?" another woman chimed in.

Fang-yuan turned to the speaker. "It's called sacrifice."

"I wouldn't use that word," Pan-pan said, eyeing Shui-lian, who had finally managed to close the bag. "The way I see it, we came here together and we're leaving as a pair as well."

"But where will you go?" Elder Sister Meng asked again. "Home?"

"Not home," said Shui-lian quickly. "We're off to the capital. Pan-pan has a contact there. We're going to find her—and better jobs than this."

"You are both brave girls," Elder Sister Meng commented, smiling. Bending over, she dragged an empty washbasin from under a bunk. Before she set it on the floor in front of her, she dropped in a twenty-yuan note.

"*Man zou*—go with care," she said softly, then left the room.

By the time Pan-pan and Shui-lian were ready to leave, the basin was more than half full of crumpled bills. After a final goodbye to everyone in the dorm, and one last look at the bare bunk, they headed toward the door.

"Wait!" someone called out.

It was Fang-yuan. She gave each of the two friends a bone-crushing hug. "Goodbye, cousins," she said, smiling, her eyes brimming with tears.

Two guards, leaning against the door frame of the hut, watched them approach. One frowned; the other just shrugged his shoulders. The guards saw workers coming and going all the time. While all the new arrivals brought different dreams and expectations, every departing worker acted more or less the same, crushed and defeated. Many had to be hauled out of their dorms, dragged across the compound, and thrown out the door, their belongings tossed after them over the closed gate.

But the scene they were witnessing today was something

entirely different. One of the girls had a dirty sling on her chest. There were no tears, or angry shouts. They looked almost triumphant as they walked past the gatehouse. They didn't stop or turn their heads when the gate was pushed shut with a loud clunk.

柳暗花明又一村

Part Three

Liu an hua ming you yi cun

In the shadow of a willow
wildflowers glow.
A village comes in view.

Chapter Twenty-One

When Shui-lian opened her eyes, she saw, through the train window, the pale light of early morning illuminating the landscape. Trucks and carts drawn by horses and donkeys were lined up at the rail crossings as the train sped past, its horn a long, mournful cry. Gradually, the orderly cultivated fields yielded to paved roads that grew wider and longer by the minute. In the distance, the roads appeared in stacks, one on top of another. A few merged with the sky at the horizon. Shui-lian realized that these must be the freeways Pan-pan had talked about, like the one that her father had been labouring on for years. Alongside the tracks, the simple, sparse dwellings gave way to tall buildings that kept growing larger and soaring higher.

Then the train began to slow down, reducing its speed to that of a turtle as it crawled to a halt. "Beijing Central Station!" the conductor declared.

Slinging their bedrolls onto their backs and their canvas bags across their shoulders, Pan-pan and Shui-lian stepped down from the train and trailed after a stream of passengers toward the exit. The air was hot and dry. Their plastic sandals felt like dough, warm and soft against their bare soles as they moved along the sun-baked platform and into the station. Finally, they stopped in the centre of an enormous circular hall, where they were surrounded by the echoing din of thousands of voices and moving feet. Dozens of large colour-TV monitors mounted on the walls showed not pictures but lines of text.

Pan-pan put down her bedroll, leaning it against her leg. She wiped the sweat from her forehead with her shirt sleeve, letting her eyes devour everything in front of her: the smooth, shining marble floor that must feel cool and heavenly if she were allowed to lie on it; the giant lamps dangling in the corners, suspended from the towering ceiling—lamps that could brighten the entire place like the crystal palace at the bottom of the Eastern Sea, she thought, recalling a fairy tale she had loved hearing her mother tell.

Shui-lian's wandering eyes fixed on a pair of moving staircases, one carrying people up, the other bringing them down—all so effortlessly—and probably a lot of fun. From the look of it, the ride was free. She pulled Pan-pan along beside her to the moving steps. They rode, laughing, up and down three times before they reluctantly got off and headed for the station's main exit.

Out in the square, Pan-pan reminded herself that they had better ask how to get to Sun Ming's place or they might end up having nowhere to spend the night and the days to come. After a furious discussion, in which Shui-lian wouldn't give in to Pan-pan's suggestion that they look for a policeman, Shui-lian pointed to a middle-aged woman shouting at the top of her lungs, selling maps.

"How about her?"

"One yuan," the woman said to Shui-lian, peeling a sheet from a thick stack draped over her outstretched forearm.

"Fine, Auntie," Pan-pan answered before Shui-lian had a chance to, reaching inside her pocket. "But first, could you help us find a certain street? We're new in Beijing."

"Tell me quick," the woman grumbled. "I have to sell a hundred of these maps a day, the entire stack, to make a profit."

"It's Chaoyangmen—Chao-yang Gate," Pan-pan said without hesitation, for she had memorized that part of Sun Ming's address long ago.

"*Aiya,* typical *wai-di-ren,*" the map-seller cried out. *Wai-di-ren* referred to someone who wasn't a local, but Pan-pan knew it could be a put-down, meaning a country bumpkin. As soon as she saw Shui-lian's face darken, a prelude to an outburst, she grabbed her elbow. Quickly she added, "Please help us."

"Whereabouts on Chaoyangmen?" the woman demanded impatiently. "There are lots of places named after the Gate of the Rising Sun. First of all, there's Chaoyangmen District. As for the streets, there are Inner Chaoyangmen Avenue and Outer Chaoyangmen Avenue, Northern Chaoyangmen Road and Southern Chaoyangmen Road. So which one are you looking for?"

When she saw Pan-pan take a piece of paper out of her bag, the woman snatched it from her hand. "Now we're getting somewhere," she sighed.

"You know where it is?" Pan-pan chirped anxiously, her eyes flashing. "I hope it's not too far."

"I know where it is all right, or should I say, where it used to be."

"What do you mean?" Shui-lian cut in finally. "It's a place, not a piece of ice that may have melted on a hot day like this. The street couldn't have just disappeared, could it?"

"It has disappeared, young woman. Don't you understand what's happening in this city?" The map-seller raised her voice again, but this time Shui-lian could tell that the woman's anger was not directed at her. Tapping Sun Ming's address with her finger, the map-seller went on. "The whole area was levelled not long ago to build fancy hotels. Now the damned Olympics!" she spat. "Ever since the announcement, everything in the city is subjected to the Olympic Games. When the time comes, the government wants to pretend to the rest of the world that China is as rich as the West."

The woman rattled on, not realizing that most of her words, in particular the reference to the Olympics, were going straight over Shui-lian's head.

"But what happened to the people who used to live there?" Pan-pan asked when the map-seller finally decided to catch a breath. "We don't care about what's going on there. We just want to find this person."

"Gone," the woman replied, lashing her free hand into the air.

"Gone?" Pan-pan stumbled. "Where? All of them? Are you sure? How ...?"

"If you don't believe me, go check it out yourself," the woman scolded and began to shout. "Map! Get your Beijing map!"

"Wait, Auntie. At least tell us how to get there," Pan-pan pleaded. All the expectations she had harboured since she decided to leave the factory were threatening to evaporate.

"That's what the map's for!" the woman snapped. Shaking her head, she took a pen out of her pocket and circled an intersection within a maze of criss-crossed lanes on Pan-pan's map. "Here's where we are." She then moved the tip of the pen upward and drew a square over a web of thin lines. "Here's the area where your relative lives, or used to. These thin lines are *hu-tongs,* the residential alleyways. Most are gone now. Some are still being demolished. You'll see for yourself." She pointed north with her free hand, and her voice softened. "Walk straight and pass ..." she stopped, looking up at a hazy sky and counting in murmurs, "pass seven, maybe eight streets, I'm not sure anymore. Anyway, you won't miss it. It's the second wide street next to Changan Avenue. Cross on your left and walk a few more blocks before heading north again. *Aiya,* why am I telling you all this? It's a wasteland now. A ruin. You can't miss it."

Chapter Twenty-Two

Fifteen minutes later, after saying goodbye to the cranky map-seller, Pan-pan and Shui-lian reached Changan Avenue, the Avenue of Eternal Peace, the widest road either of them had ever clapped eyes on. Pan-pan peered in both directions, wondering how on earth a road could be so long and flat—and so straight, without a single turn or twist as far as her eyes could see. Standing on tiptoe, Shui-lian, too, craned her neck, gazing up and down the spacious boulevard that was broader than some of the rivers in Sichuan. Yet all six lanes were jam-packed with moving vehicles, all zipping past like blowing wind, all in a great hurry.

But nothing was as strange or scary as the discovery that there was no means to cross the thoroughfare. Each corner of the sidewalk was fenced off by metal bars. If it hadn't been for a kind old man who directed them to an underground passage, Pan-pan and Shui-lian would have been stranded there for a long time. When they re-emerged on the north side of the boulevard, Pan-pan stopped to check the map and realized that the famous Tiananmen Square was only blocks away. So was the Forbidden City, the residence of the Chinese emperors and their families that her mother had talked about so often when Pan-pan was a child. Thinking about her mother, Pan-pan was engulfed by an aching homesickness. After almost three months of living in a walled compound, Beijing's busy streets, the towering buildings, and the throngs of people made her yearn for her village and her home in Guizhou, for Ah-Po's cooking, even Xin-Ma's chirpiness, and the shrieks of little Gui-yang. In the past three months she had written home twice and received one letter from Xin-Ma, which she had kept from Shui-lian, as her friend had heard nothing from her family in Sichuan. Pan-pan planned to write again as soon as she located Sun Ming. The last time she heard from them, her half-brother was learning to talk. By now he had probably become a chatterbox like his mother. The rising heat and constant din that wrapped around her like a thick blanket also stirred memories of cool mountain air, even in the midst of summer, and tranquility. The twisting trails and footpaths she had disliked for as long as she could remember seemed enchanting now.

As she and Shui-lian plodded wordlessly along the hot pavement, Pan-pan didn't want to think about where they would spend the night if they failed to find Sun Ming. Nevertheless, the worry hung in her mind and refused to leave.

Beside her, Shui-lian paused to loosen the shoulder straps of her bedroll. It was getting heavier, leaving a large soggy patch on her back. As she trudged along beside Pan-pan, she didn't understand how Beijing—Northern Capital—could be this hot. She wished there was a river nearby, even a pond, that she could jump into to cool herself, as she had often done as a child. And she was thirsty and hungry. The throbbing pain from her wound and the insistent buzzing of cicadas in the trees made her head spin. She wished time would stop. If she were alone, she would plunk herself down right in the middle of the sidewalk, stretch out, close her eyes, and try to ignore the heat, the noise, and the endless flow of people.

Following the map, Pan-pan led Shui-lian onto Inner Chaoyangmen Avenue. A few blocks farther west they crossed the road onto North Chaoyangmen Road. Immediately they found themselves facing a field of ruins. It looked as though an earthquake had struck, with the piles of debris, mounds of broken bricks and clay roof tiles, heaps of severed wooden posts and beams. Like battered curbs, the wall foundations mapped a whole neighbourhood of single-storey houses, courtyards, and *hu-tongs* that had once existed. Two giant yellow machines were working in the distance, growling and puffing black smoke. Each was armed with a long steel claw, slowly yet determinedly clearing the ground. A mere touch of the claw, it appeared, and everything standing in its way was toppled, as though the clay and brick structures as well as the concrete walls were all made of toy blocks. Clouds of dust rose and mingled with the quivering heat, tangling and dancing together. It was a scene of desolation and despair, a ghost town under a bright sunny sky, a sharp contrast with what they'd just witnessed: the vast tree-lined boulevards, the glittering glass and steel high-rises and apartment buildings.

As she looked about, Pan-pan felt anxious and confused. How could a neighbourhood vanish? The area was, by the look of it, at least several times larger than her village, and had been home to so many people, including Sun Ming. Where were they? They couldn't have just disappeared like the swirling dust. Even dust, Pan-pan thought, would eventually have to settle somewhere.

Pan-pan felt overcome by desperation. Where would she start her search for Sun Ming? She had failed Shui-lian again, dragged her all the way north to this wasteland. Another futile mission, like fetching water in a bamboo basket. First the factory, now this. By the look of it, Sun Ming could be anywhere, maybe not even in the city anymore. Pan-pan didn't have a clue where to go from here, nor enough money to go home even if she and Shui-lian wanted to.

"Everything's gone," she said. "It's hopeless!"

"Look, Pan-pan," said Shui-lian, pointing into the sun. "What about that house?"

As a hot breeze parted the dust, a low wall, then the house behind it, came into view. The house's black clay tile roof was still intact. Shielding her eyes against the sun with her hand, Pan-pan squinted harder and saw a chimney.

"Good," she said with relief. "It looks like people still live there. Let's go and see."

Gingerly, they picked their way forward, circling heaps of splintered wood and shards of plaster and mortar, passing dismantled furniture and broken household items, skipping over puddles of black water and ditches filled with soiled red and green plastic bags. The whole place smelled of manure and urine and seemed to have become a haven for rats, stray dogs and cats, and swarms of redheaded flies.

As they got closer, Shui-lian realized she was looking at a damaged courtyard. Two side walls had been reduced to mounds of bricks. Half of the doorway and the back wall remained standing like defiant warriors on a battlefield. On the left, a dwelling stood almost intact, though its wooden door and window frames were all askew, vibrating and trembling in rhythm with the digging and demolition going on nearby. It must take a will of steel to live here in the midst of such chaos, thought Shui-lian. No wonder all the windows and doors were tightly shut and the curtains pulled closed despite the high temperature. From the corner of her eye she saw the curtain twitch.

"Someone's in the house," she whispered into Pan-pan's ear so that Pan-pan could hear her above the din. "Maybe they know where Sun Ming is."

"I don't think so. We're already too far away from Sun Ming's street," Pan-pan snapped, fingering the map, irritated by the heat and noise. "We're in the wrong place. Remember, she should be in an apartment building, on the third floor, not a one-storey house like this."

"It doesn't mean we shouldn't go and ask," Shui-lian lashed back. "Besides, what's the right place in such a wasteland? You tell me!"

"You're right, let's try anyway."

They headed to the door. As they got nearer, they could hear the hum of an air conditioner. Before they had a chance to knock, the crooked door opened with a sharp squeak, letting out a gust of cool, damp air and revealing a sliver of black cloth and half an unshaved face.

"What do you want?" a man croaked, clearing his throat coarsely. "Go away!"

Behind him someone was talking.

"We, we're looking for … for a relative," Pan-pan answered, using the word the map-seller had applied to Sun Ming. "She used to live here, or very near. I wonder if you know her and can tell us where she is now."

The man, who had been about to shut the door, burst out laughing. "What do you think this is? A bloody police station?" He coughed again, spat on the ground, and smeared the gob with his shoe before shutting the door in Pan-pan's face.

Pan-pan and Shui-lian stared at each other, then slowly turned and walked out of the courtyard. By now the sun had climbed higher, and the pounding and smashing had stopped. The site was strangely quiet. The crew must be having their morning break. Hot, thirsty, hungry, and utterly discouraged, Pan-pan and Shui-lian found a pool of shade behind the wall and sat down. Leaning against their bedrolls, they ate some leftover dry bread, each immersed in her own thoughts, then they both fell asleep.

When they awoke, the sun had shifted and was now baking them in its fading glory. The machines had moved to the other side of the ruins, and sounds from the streets floated in: the shouts of Popsicle-sellers, the ringing of bicycle bells, and the constantly beeping horns of cars and trucks.

Shui-lian yawned and stretched her arms. "I need to go to the toilet," she said, standing up.

"Me too. I wonder if there's one nearby."

To their surprise, they found one just around the corner, and it was open. And open was all it was. Where the door and windows had once been, holes gaped in the decrepit walls. Even before they walked in, the stench made their eyes water. According to the blue-and-white plate hanging above the entrance, the facility had been set up for the use of local residents who didn't have indoor plumbing. It was simply a large room, with low partitions between each hole that served as a toilet. The place must have seen much better days, and smelled better, Shui-lian thought, holding her breath as she ducked her head low to avoid the clouds of buzzing flies that protested her intrusion.

Once outside again, they spotted a water tap on a pipe sticking out of the ground. Taking turns, they bent down, splashing cold water on their faces and drinking from their scooped palms.

"Are you tired of living?" a voice demanded. "Some folks won't even let their dogs drink that."

The same man they had encountered earlier stood behind them, holding two plastic pails.

"We're thirsty," Pan-pan grumbled.

"Then go buy some bottled water like everyone else does nowadays," the man scolded, setting one pail under the tap.

"If we could afford to buy bottled water, we wouldn't be here, wandering in this stinky dump," Shui-lian muttered.

"I'm not in the mood for a sad story, okay? Save it for another day, or for someone else," he shot back, yet his voice had softened a bit. Turning off the tap, he asked, "Where are you from, anyway?"

"Guizhou," Pan-pan replied.

"I'm from Sichuan," added Shui-lian. A sense of rightness filled her heart as soon as she heard herself say those words loud and clear after three months of pretence and hiding.

"You've both travelled a long way," the man replied. Now clean-shaven and wearing a white T-shirt, he seemed to be a different person altogether. In the natural light, he looked younger, even though he was going bald. "I spent six years of my youth in Sichuan. Unwillingly, mind you." He paused, giving Shui-lian a faint smile. "If I try really hard, I might still be able to speak with your accent."

Lao Feng, as he asked them to call him, lived with his widowed mother. Six months ago she had suffered a stroke, which had paralyzed her left side. "She fell ill just two days after we were given the notice of eviction," he said.

From Lao Feng, Pan-pan and Shui-lian learned that the family compound, or *si-he-yuan*—four-walled courtyard—was typical Beijing housing. It normally contained three houses, thus three families. Each house was built against one of three walls, with the fourth wall, facing the alleyway and equipped with a double door, serving as the entrance. The enclosed yard was where the three families did their washing and cooking and relaxing. "Our lane is called Horseshoe Hu-tong. Most of the houses were constructed during the Qing Dynasty, more than a hundred years ago," Lao Feng explained as the three of them walked, heading slowly in the direction of his courtyard.

"These *si-he-yuan* neighbourhoods are a Beijing specialty. They reflect our history, culture, and heritage," Lao Feng continued, his voice betraying a hint of anger. "Three years ago, a wealthy Hong Kong developer purchased the whole area. His plan was to demolish every old building to make room for fancy hotels and shopping malls. And the government agreed. As a result, every resident has been ordered to leave and live somewhere else."

"But why do you want to live in an old house when you've been offered a new one?" Shui-lian asked when she finally had a chance, recalling the tall and stylish apartment blocks lining the streets that she had seen earlier. "Even I can tell they're a hundred times better than your place."

Lao Feng halted and gave Shui-lian a look that had become familiar to her since she had left home, then smiled. "You really don't know how the whole thing works, do you?" He emptied the pails of water into the cistern beside his damaged house. "As soon as we agree to leave, sign our names on the piece of paper, we say goodbye to the place. I don't mean just our house, but downtown Beijing. We'll end up living in a faraway suburb. Most of us who used to have homes here can't afford the kind of apartments you've seen. The money we were offered as compensation can't even buy a hallway or section of staircase in the high-rises you've mentioned. Only the super-rich can afford them."

Pan-pan couldn't help butting in. "But that would be like buying your own house back at a much higher price!" She tried to imagine how Ah-Po and Dad and Xin-Ma would react if they were forced to leave their home and were never allowed to live in Yunxi Village again. "And where are your neighbours now?" she asked.

"Gone. All scattered around like worthless dirt. Most of them are in the new suburbs, far away from schools, workplaces, and hospitals. The government calls it fair compensation, but I call it robbery in broad daylight." His voice broke. "And even if I was willing, what about my mother? She has to get treatment twice a week at the Traditional Chinese Medicine Hospital, which is two streets away from here. If we move, how can I get her there? Thirty kilometres each way? All I have is my old tank of a bike, and I have to work two jobs to support her, her medical costs, and myself."

Pan-pan and Shui-lian looked awkwardly at each other. If earlier they had convinced themselves that they were the only poor souls wandering the streets of this glorious city, they now both realized they were wrong.

"Listen." Lao Feng spoke again, breaking the stillness. "If you have no place to stay while looking for your relative, I can put you up for a couple of days."

"Really?" Pan-pan exclaimed.

Beside her, Shui-lian averted her eyes, shifting her feet uneasily. "Let's talk about it first," she hissed to Pan-pan from behind clenched teeth.

"Do you have a better place in mind?" Pan-pan shot back.

"Listen," Lao Feng broke in. "You two think about it. But let me make it clear. I am willing to put you up for a few days, but not inside the house." He looked directly at Shui-lian. "We have only two small bedrooms, and my mother needs her rest." Pointing to the open space between the house and the remains of the wall he added, "Over there. You can move the stuff out and clear a spot. I have an old tent my parents bought many years ago after the Tangshan earthquake. I can set it up for you if you want."

"Oh, thank you so much," Pan-pan said, nudging Shui-lian with her elbow.

"Yes. It's very kind of you," Shui-lian replied, forcing a smile.

"Don't get too excited," said Lao Feng, "I'm not offering you a five-star hotel. Besides, it's an exchange, if you agree. I'd like you to keep an eye on my mother when I'm at work. I have two jobs, both part time. I'm a traffic controller. That's a fancy title for someone holding a red pennant, standing in a busy intersection during rush hour. A new effort to force drivers, cyclists, and pedestrians to obey the traffic rules. I'm also a night watchman on a construction site for a new sports complex, guarding the building materials. My mother's recovering slowly but steadily thanks to acupuncture and other traditional treatments. She's able to speak again and move around a bit in her wheelchair, but from time to time she still needs help. Does that sound okay with you two?"

"Yes," Pan-pan and Shui-lian chirped at the same time. "But—"

Lao Feng put up his hand and interrupted Pan-pan. "I can't promise you anything with regard to finding your relative. Do you know how many people used to live here? Tens of thousands. Finding her will be like searching for a sewing needle on the bottom of the ocean. But I'll ask around. That's all I can do."

Chapter Twenty-Three

Pan-pan and Shui-lian stood quietly, watching with fascination as Lao Feng set up the blue tent on the cleared patch of ground next to the house. They crawled inside to spread out their bedding, and, looking around, giggled. The tent was large enough for four people to lie down. It heated up quickly, but they felt as contented as if they were in paradise. Just the two of them, away from strangers and probing eyes. What novelty! Earlier, Lao Feng had insisted they come into the house and have something to eat, out of the heat for a while. There they met his mother, a white-haired old woman who insisted on feeding herself, using a spoon to scoop the rice into her mouth, half of which fell onto the table.

Before Lao Feng left for work that evening, he gave his mother a brass bell to ring in case she needed help. The pear-shaped bell reminded Pan-pan of the one her teacher had used for recess and for resuming classes at the village school. This one produced an intense clang that Pan-pan assured Lao Feng they'd hear easily.

Pan-pan and Shui-lian thanked Lao Feng for the food and the flashlight he offered and went outside. Darkness was slowly falling, yet the heat lingered, refusing to depart. Pan-pan and Shui-lian sat down on a broken roof beam facing the ruins, listening to the noise of the city in the background.

Shui-lian lifted her face, staring at a vast sky mapped with stars. It reminded her of her days on the water, which she had come to miss more than she ever thought she would. Thinking about home, she felt tears well up in her eyes. What would my mother say if someone told her I was sitting outside a broken house among rubble and garbage in downtown Beijing, looking at the same sky and stars she sees above the deck of the family boat? What would she do if she learned that three months away from home I had lost half a thumb? Shui-lian hadn't heard one word from her family. How could she? She wondered if Jin-lin had gone back to see her mother yet, or if her family had tried to find her. She lowered her eyes, nervously surveying the shadows between the heaps of bricks near and far.

Lao Feng had assured them that they had no need to worry about their safety staying outdoors. Because of the demolition and chaos, this was one of the safest places in the city: No one in his right mind would bother to come here, even if he were invited.

Nevertheless, Shui-lian still had a hard time falling sleep, even after Pan-pan offered to take the spot nearest the tent's opening. Eventually she drifted off. But she soon woke up screaming, feeling something fumbling at her thin cotton trousers. All the fear and horror she had tried to repress rushed back. She twisted to get herself free, frantically flapping her good hand to defend herself, shouting at the top of her lungs, "They're here! They're here again!"

Pan-pan jerked awake. She rolled over, stroking her friend's forehead and murmuring that no one else was in the tent, that

Shui-lian was safe. When Shui-lian quieted and slipped back to sleep, Pan-pan reached for the flashlight. She gasped when the beam caught a pair of tiny red eyes glaring at her.

After a moment's hesitation, the rat skittered away, reluctantly leaving behind a mess of crumbs from a dried bun Shui-lian had left in her pocket. The scene reminded Pan-pan of the days at Niavia. Although rats were no strangers to Pan-pan, she hadn't expected to see them in the factory, still less travelling in groups in broad daylight, inside the workshops and dorms. Worse still, their overgrowing population had attracted snakes, which crawled freely into the compound from the nearby fields. Most, after a feast of rat, would slither away again. But a few stayed, coiling up under the sewing machines and cutting tables, ready to send the workers running away in panic.

Early the next morning, light infiltrated the mesh windows of the tent. Shui-lian trailed Pan-pan into the house, wondering for the first time if she had made a mistake, following Pan-pan here, instead of going somewhere else. Lao Feng wasn't home yet from his night job, so they helped his mother out of her bed and into her wheelchair. In her faltering manner of speaking, she asked Pan-pan and Shui-lian to call her *Da-Ma*—Elder Mother—and insisted they sit down and have breakfast with her.

As Shui-lian was preparing the food, Pan-pan looked around her. The house was divided into two sections. Half of the main room was taken up by a sofa and two big chairs, opposite a TV set. A square table and a few wooden seats dominated the other half. Two closet-like bedrooms made up the back of the house.

Through the side window, Pan-pan could see a small shed in the corner of the yard—the washing place, she guessed.

Shui-lian and Pan-pan sat down to a meal of cold rice porridge, boiled eggs, and shredded pickled vegetables. Afterward, with the dishes done and the floor swept, Pan-pan told Da-Ma that she and Shui-lian would be outside in the yard. If she needed them, she should just ring the bell. Da-Ma nodded but kept murmuring, "It's hot outside. Too noisy. Too dusty."

The sun was up now, the sky a burst of light. The temperature was rising fast, indicating another scorching day ahead. Shui-lian shaded her eyes with her good hand, squinting toward the direction where the grinding and shattering were already underway, funnels of dust rolling in clouds.

"Pan-pan, I'm going to gather some bricks to weigh down the bottom edges of the tent walls and prevent rats from getting in again. Besides, I'm afraid it might be blown away in a thunderstorm." She made a wide sweep with her arm. "There are enough bricks here in the yard. It won't take me long."

Shui-lian was afraid that if she remained sitting next to Pan-pan, she might admit to her friend that she was feeling depressed and missed her home and family. Earlier, when she opened her eyes and saw the tent's filmy blue walls, she thought for a moment she was back home, under the awning of her family boat. Her heart had filled with a sense of happiness and relief. Minutes later, the desolation surrounding the tent reminded her of the harsh reality of their situation, the bleakness of the odds of finding Sun Ming, let alone a job. She and Pan-pan had listened to Lao Feng talk about his search for work, tramping from one place to another. Shui-lian wondered about her chance of ever making a living in the capital. Who would hire her—even if she still had two whole thumbs, which she didn't? She couldn't live in a tent for the rest of her life, even if she was allowed. What would happen to them if they ran out of money? There were too many questions, but not even one answer. She needed to be busy, to keep her mind off these worries and her homesickness, or she might break down in front of Pan-pan, who had made such a sacrifice for her.

Of all the things scattered among the wreckage—the toys, the clothes, the broken furniture and other household items—what had caught Shui-lian's eye was the loose bricks lying all over the place. Most were shattered, but many were still whole. And judging from the way the workers were going, all the bricks, as well as everything else on the ground, would soon be scooped up, dumped into trucks, and carted away. She couldn't help feeling sad and angry. When she was a child, she often heard her father and mother and other river *ku-lis* talk about their dreams of living in a house with a strong roof and solid walls. Years later, it was that longing that had led her into the hands of Da-Ge. Here, surrounded by a field of jumbled blue-grey bricks and black roof tiles, she wished she could take all of them home, whole or broken, to build a house for herself and her family on the bank of the Jialing River.

"Good idea," Pan-pan responded. "How about letting me collect them? You stay here and keep an ear open for Lao Feng's mother. I don't want your hand to get infected."

"Don't worry about my hand. It's healing," Shui-lian said, swinging the sling to make her point. "I'm afraid if I sit around any longer I'll have calluses on my bum."

They set to work right away, picking through a mound around the skeletal remains of the doorway. Shui-lian lifted a brick, shook it free of dust, and tucked it under her left arm. She then took up another one in her free hand and walked back to the tent, where she placed the bricks so as to hold down the tent's skirt. Slowly a low barrier, two bricks high, formed around the tent.

As the morning wore on, without meaning to, the two of them had put up a little wall, extending out of Lao Feng's courtyard.

"What are you two doing? Building the Olympic Village?"

Pan-pan and Shui-lian straightened up and found Lao Feng standing behind them, shaking his head and laughing.

"Oh, I'm sorry, Lao Feng," Pan-pan apologized. "We got carried away. Did we miss Da-Ma's call?"

"No, no, nothing like that. My mother is fine." Lao Feng stopped chuckling, but his eyes still danced. "Wow, herringbone style!" he added, cocking his head to take a closer look at the wall, now about half a metre tall and two and a half metres long, winding through the rubble. "A miniature of the Great Wall!" he said cheerily, squatting on his heels and examining one of the curves. "Where did you two learn such a skill?"

"Not me. She did it," Shui-lian said, wiping the sweat from her forehead.

"It's not a big deal," Pan-pan said with a shy smile. "Everyone in my village knows how to put up a wall in this way, including kids."

When Pan-pan was a child she had watched her parents and Ah-Po at the laborious task of making mud bricks, the only kind of bricks they could afford. First, Dad would trudge to the mountainside with a shoulder pole and two large pails. There he dug earth with a hoe and carried the dirt home. No one in the village would even think of using the precious earth from the terraced fields. As Dad made trip after trip, the brown soil accumulated in a pile. At the same time, Mom and Ah-Po were busy chopping rice straw into two-centimetre lengths, to be mixed with the dirt before water was added. More mixing, and endless beating and pounding with heavy spades. On warm days, Mom would take off her shoes and socks and trample the mixture with her bare feet, until straw and earth were well blended into a thick paste. Dad would then carefully scoop the paste into a row of wooden moulds. Hours later—if it happened to be a good drying day—Pan-pan's mother would gingerly nudge the moulds free one by one. Dad taught young Pan-pan how to stack the bricks, once they were hard enough to be picked up, in rows, in a herringbone pattern that allowed them to dry further without crushing one another. Unless the bricks were properly hardened, he warned young Pan-pan, anything built with them would collapse.

While Pan-pan had no clear idea why she and Shui-lian were putting up a wall in the midst of a ruin, she was as baffled as Shui-lian why these bricks, which the farmers in the village would have loved to have, were treated like worthless trash. How could she express her anger to the man who was so kind as to give them a place to stay, and who might help them find Sun Ming?

"We're bored sitting around. We just want to do something," was all she ended up saying.

Lao Feng stood up. "I understand. But it's getting too hot. Why don't you take a break? I'm home now. Link Plaza is just around the corner. Go and have a look, and cool yourselves down. The entire place is air-conditioned." He took some money out of his pocket and handed it to Pan-pan. "Go. Buy some ice cream. My treat."

"No, we can't take your money," Pan-pan said.

"We'll go," Shui-lian cut in. "But we have our own money."

Chapter Twenty-Four

Link Plaza was a huge shopping mall that took up the corner of a block. Shui-lian and Pan-pan approached a bank of glass doors, the one in the centre revolving mindlessly. Behind it a hall stretched as wide as a street, flanked with glittering windows filled with outlandish clothing; shoes and sandals with spike heels; exquisitely shaped bottles of coloured liquid; soaps, and shampoos, and hair oils; beds jammed with pillows and cushions of all forms and sizes; shiny pots and pans and many other cooking utensils and machines. The place smelled like flowers and candies. No wonder it was called Link Plaza, Pan-pan said to herself: store after store, just like links on a chain. The second floor held an expansive food court, the source of the exotic aromas that hovered overhead. The mall was cool and spacious compared with the hot and crowded streets outside. Pan-pan and Shui-lian walked slowly, savouring the pleasant change of atmosphere, sliding and skidding playfully on the floor's smooth surface and passing shop after shop.

Shui-lian halted suddenly, her eyes drawn to the display window of a clothing store before her. It wasn't the sheer, colourful summer dresses that attracted her attention. She found herself looking at a young woman wearing worn pants and a soiled shirt, with one sleeve rolled up above the elbow and the other inside a dirty sling hung across her chest. The woman gazed back at her through familiar eyes. Her eyes, but sadder and less determined than she was used to. How out of place I look, Shui-lian thought. Surrounded by stylish, costly garments and glittering lights, I'm more like an alien from another planet. Moving closer, Shui-lian tilted her head to the left, then to the right, studying the reflection, willing it to be someone else.

Turning to leave, she spotted herself in the side window of the same store and in the shop window across the aisle. As she quickened her steps to catch up with Pan-pan, the same image followed her along the shiny marble walls.

"Pan-pan, look. It's you over there, and down here," she called out excitedly, pointing at the marble floor.

"I've noticed it," Pan-pan said cheerfully. "It's kind of weird, seeing ourselves everywhere we turn, like we were movie stars. Talking about stars," she went on, pointing to a clothing store called *Xiao-ge-zi*—Petite—across the hall, "see the red dress in the window? What a beautiful colour! It reminds me of wild fire. You know what, Shui-lian, I bet it would look ten times better on you than on that pale, yellow-haired mannequin. Let's go and take a closer look."

"What for? I could never afford it." The colour reminded Shui-lian of the sweater her mother had knitted for her.

"Who said we have to buy it? It'll cost us nothing to look at it. It's called window-shopping. Besides," Pan-pan giggled, "how can they tell? There are no words on our faces saying that we have no money. Come on, we're in a mall, not the Niavia compound. We're free to go in and walk around."

Inside the store, every light was on, as if in competition with the midday sun pouring through the side windows. Half the floor was taken up by rows of racks packed with shirts, pants, dresses, and skirts. Wooden shelves lined the walls, each stacked from top to bottom with folded garments. Shoppers browsed, flipping through hanger after hanger before moving to the next rack. In one corner, a stylish young woman stood in front of a full-length mirror holding a floral dress against herself, tilting her head from side to side.

Pan-pan spotted the red dresses like the one she had seen in the window on a rack at the back. Eyes bright and faces gleaming, the girls made a full circle around it, marvelling at the soft material.

"It even has a lining," Shui-lian whispered to Pan-pan, lifting the bottom hem with the fingertips of her good hand. "The same shade of red, see—"

"What do you think you're doing?" A stern voice rose sharply. Shui-lian quickly withdrew her hand. Pan-pan turned her head to find a clerk glowering at them.

"If you've caused any damage you'll have to buy it," the woman asserted, stepping forward and pushing Shui-lian out of her way.

"How can we cause any damage by merely touching it?" Pan-pan argued. "Like everyone else is doing?"

"You're not everyone else. Your hands are dirty," the clerk shot back. "Take a look at your hands and fingernails—the two of you. They're black and filthy. With hands like those, you're not allowed to touch anything here. What have you been doing, anyway? Digging ditches with your bare hands? This store isn't for people like you."

"Let's go, Pan-pan," Shui-lian urged, pulling Pan-pan's shirt and refusing to make eye contact with the clerk. "We don't belong here."

"That's right," the woman snarled. "And find a place to clean your hands."

"Not until we use them to dig a grave for you," Pan-pan said calmly.

"Sh! Pan-pan! You'll get us into trouble," Shui-lian hissed, pulling Pan-pan out of the store. "I'm the one who should have told her that."

"Who says?" Pan-pan replied, laughing.

"Look, Pan-pan, I don't want to stay here any longer. Let's go back."

"Back where?" Pan-pan said with alarm, stopping in the middle of the mall. "You're not giving up already, are you? What am I going to do without you?"

"What are you talking about?" Shui-lian cut her off. "I meant go back to Lao Feng's place."

Pan-pan broke into a smile. "You scared me. I thought you meant go back to Sichuan. All right, let's go. We can build the wall some more."

"Yes," Shui-lian said, taking one last look at herself in a shop window before she led Pan-pan back the way they had come and strode out onto the street.

OVER THE NEXT TWO DAYS, as the wall grew longer, word spread through the neighbourhood. Many people came to take a look at what the two young women were doing. Most of them stood around, chatting and pointing at Shui-lian and Pan-pan and commenting on their handiwork. Some marvelled at their patience and skill, and told them so; others laughed, shaking their heads as they wandered off. The entire demolition crew even walked over to see the wall during their break. Some shrugged their shoulders; some looked at one another bewildered before returning to their work. Even Lao Feng's mother seemed to sense something was going on outside her house. She beamed each time she saw Pan-pan and Shui-lian.

As she worked on the wall, Shui-lian withdrew into her thoughts. Her brief, humbling experience at Link Plaza proved that she didn't belong in Beijing, with its traffic and noise; its soaring, gleaming buildings; and its people who, like the clerk in the clothing store, seemed so knowing and worldly. How could she, a river girl, ever fit in? What kind of future could she look forward to, dressed in rags, with a grimy face and blackened hands? The girl I saw reflected in the storefront glass, she told herself, could never be a part of modern city life.

And Shanghai, people said, was even more fast-paced and sophisticated. How had she ever imagined there would be a place for her? She should be back on the boat with her family. No one could say she hadn't tried. Not even her mother. Maybe she'll change her mind and not force me to marry the old boatman, she thought. But what was she going to say to Pan-pan, the friend who had been so loyal to her?

Shui-lian sat down on a broken wall foundation, watching Pan-pan carefully stack the bricks the way her father had taught her. Sliding her arm from the sling, Shui-lian pulled the dusty cloth over her head and, using her unbandaged hand, worked the knot free. She smoothed the cloth on her knees, then folded it and stuffed it in her pocket. I'll tell Pan-pan tonight, she decided.

"PAN-PAN, THERE'S SOMETHING I need to talk to you about," Shui-lian said. It was late afternoon on their third day camped in Lao Feng's yard, and they were about to quit for the day. The wall was getting closer to the busy street, but neither Shui-lian nor Pan-pan had mentioned one word about what they would do when there were no bricks left.

Pan-pan rose, her back to the lowering sun. Shui-lian walked over and stood next to Pan-pan, screwing up her courage to tell her friend her decision. But Pan-pan spoke first.

"It really does look like the Great Wall, doesn't it?" she said. "The way it twists and turns."

"I don't know. I've never seen the Great Wall."

"I haven't either, but my mother showed me pictures. Maybe someday we'll have a chance to see it with our own eyes, since it's not far from here. Anyway, what is it you want to talk about?"

"Well," Shui-lian began, "I—"

"Hey! Hello! You girls, hello!"

Pan-pan and Shui-lian turned in the direction of the voice and saw a middle-aged woman heading toward them from the street.

"Were you calling us, Auntie?" Pan-pan asked.

"Yes, I was," the woman replied pleasantly. "Where are you two from?"

"Who wants to know?" Shui-lian asked, annoyed by the interruption. Probably another nosy, useless stranger who was about to offer her comments on their wall. Straightening up, she eyed the woman suspiciously. The woman wore a silk blouse and light-coloured pants. She reminded Shui-lian of Comrade Guo, the government auntie from the women's federation. She even sounded like her.

Ignoring Shui-lian's rudeness, the woman spoke again. "Okay, if you don't want to tell me that, how about giving me your names?"

"I'm from Guizhou, Auntie," Pan-pan answered, rubbing her palms together to clean off the brick dust. "Tell her, Shui-lian."

"Sichuan."

"Did you travel all the way to Beijing by yourselves?" the woman asked, sounding almost delighted. Without waiting for an answer, she turned to Pan-pan. "Where in Guizhou?"

"Yunxi Village. Why?"

"What's your name?"

"Bai Pan-pan."

The gleam that Shui-lian had seen a moment ago faded from the woman's face as she murmured, "I knew a village of the same name once, and a boy named Bai Dao-feng. But it's a popular surname in the region, and I may have remembered wrong. It was a long time ago."

Upon hearing her father's name, Pan-pan's heart leapt. Could this woman be—

"I'm Chen Shui-lian," said her friend. "I lived on the rivers of Sichuan. Now it's your turn. What's your name?"

The woman hesitated. "I know no one in Sichuan and have never been there. My name is Sun Ming, and I came here because I heard you two were looking for me. Obviously …"

"Sun Ming ..." Pan-pan slapped her hand over her mouth as if to prevent her heart from leaping out, then quickly removed it. Her eyes blinked rapidly. "Are you the girl from Beijing who came to live with my Ah-Po many years ago? Of course, you don't know me. I wasn't born yet. The boy you mentioned is my father, and you knew my mother as well. She was the little girl who, according to Ah-Po, followed you everywhere."

"Lin-fei is your mom? How could I forget her? Her parents were beaten to death by the Red Guards in the early days of the Cultural Revolution. Ah-Po was so brave to take her in."

"She is my late mother," Pan-pan murmured.

Sun Ming frowned. "Did you say 'late'?"

"Yes. Mom died three years ago."

Shui-lian's eyes darted back and forth between Pan-pan and Sun Ming, trying to make the link between the red-cheeked girl she'd heard about and this drawn and tired-looking older woman. It was hard to imagine that this was the same person who, according to Pan-pan, had been swept away from the village in a Jeep thirty years ago, laughing and calling out, "Come and see me when you're in Beijing!"

Shui-lian excused herself and headed toward the tent. She returned with Pan-pan's canvas bag and handed it to her.

"Do you remember this?" Pan-pan asked, unfolding the bag to reveal the wrinkled red star.

"Oh, my goodness, you still have it. My father gave that to me when I was sent down to the countryside. I had forgotten it until now. Your Ah-Po has kept it all these years?"

SUN MING WANTED to take the girls for a meal so that they could talk some more.

"We can't," they both said at the same time.

"Thanks, but we have to look after Da-Ma," Shui-lian added.

So the three of them sat on a broken beam in the courtyard, watching the clouds gather and the sky grow dark. Sun Ming wiped away a tear after Pan-pan's brief account of her mother's death. She clucked angrily as Shui-lian told her about her injuries and the treatment she, Pan-pan, and the other workers suffered at Niavia, and about Ah-Wu and the Demons.

"I'm sorry to hear it, girls. I don't know what else to say," she murmured, sadly shaking her head. "I've heard that the same sort of thing goes on here in Beijing. I'm glad my poor father isn't around to hear this. He was a soldier and laid down his life for the Communist Party's victory and a new China where people were free from that kind of exploitation. Now it seems our society is going backwards. It makes me so furious to think that working conditions like you've described exist in our country."

She took Shui-lian's hand in hers and looked at the soiled bandages before continuing. "I overheard someone in my restaurant talking about you two, and about the wall you've been building. It made me curious. Then one night a man walked in. I don't know him. He started asking my customers if anyone knew a woman named Sun Ming who used to live in his neighbourhood. He said it was a long shot. But my grandfather used to say that if there were no coincidences, there'd be no books, no stories, or plays. And he was right. You see, if I didn't own the restaurant, or if I hadn't overheard the man, I wouldn't have known that you were looking for me."

"Did you say you *own* the restaurant?" Shui-lian cut in. "Does that mean you're the boss?"

Sun Ming laughed. "Yes, to both questions."

"Then you must be rich and important!" Shui-lian blurted.

Sun Ming laughed again. "I wouldn't say that. But, listen," she said, glancing at her watch, "I'm afraid I have to leave now. I'll come back tomorrow to take you to my restaurant. If you don't mind my saying so, you both look like you could use a good meal or two—especially you, Shui-lian." Ignoring Shui-lian's scowl, she went on, "I also have an idea to talk over with you. Maybe you'd like to work for me?"

"You want us to cook?" Pan-pan asked.

"Not quite. Not right away, that's for sure. There are lots of other chores that need to be done in a restaurant. You'll see. I'll come by tomorrow afternoon. Meanwhile, think about it, all right?"

After they had helped Da-Ma to bed, washed the dishes, and swept the floor of the dust and grit that constantly invaded from the heaps of dirt and rubble outside, Pan-pan and Shui-lian sat by their tent, each lost in her own thoughts. The night sky was dotted with bright stars. The traffic noise had thinned out, and the street sounds had faded. But the heat lingered, and so did Sun Ming's last words. Her job offer churned in their heads.

"All my life," Shui-lian murmured, breaking the silence, "the only restaurant I ever set foot in was the one Da-Ge took Jin-lin and me to when we were supposedly on our way to Shanghai. I didn't like the place, nor can I remember what I ate. Now you and I might work in one. It makes me nervous."

"Me too. But not because it's a restaurant. It could be any place. Niavia left a sour taste in my mouth. Things have happened so quickly, all at once, which makes me uneasy. As Ah-Po would have said, once a person is bitten by a snake, she will shy away from coiled ropes for three years." Pan-pan thought a moment before she continued. "Now that I've finally met Sun Ming, seeing what she looks and sounds like, I realize that's pretty much all I know about her. Yes, I heard a lot about her when I was a kid. In my mother's eyes, Sun Ming was like a member of the family. But people change, not to mention that it was a long time ago. How can I be sure we can trust her? She sounds very nice and friendly, but will she always be good to us? After all, she's a boss."

"That's true," Shui-lian answered absently. She contemplated if it was the right time to tell Pan-pan her decision, before she was drawn into this new episode. Who could tell what further disappointments and humiliation waited for her if she stayed in Beijing any longer?

"On the other hand," Pan-pan continued, as though talking to herself, "she must be all right or she wouldn't have bothered to come here and see us, right?"

"Right," Shui-lian said loudly, to get Pan-pan's attention. "But that's all appearance. We don't know about her heart, do we? Da-Ge said kind things, too. Honey dripped from his mouth. And he smiled a lot." Shui-lian spat out her next words like they were poison. "But look what he did to me!"

"Take it easy, Shui-lian," Pan-pan soothed, alarmed at her friend's sudden distress. She moved so that she was sitting directly across from her. "Whatever Sun Ming is, she's *not* like Da-Ge or Ah-Wu. That I can tell. I'm sorry I've been so negative. I was just thinking out loud."

"But—"

"How about no buts?" Pan-pan pleaded. "How about we accept the offer? It's better than nothing. We can take one step at a time, see how it goes. If it doesn't work out, we can think about something else. The main thing is we're together. Remember the old saying: Three shoemakers working together are wiser than one scholar. Okay, there are only two of us, and we're *ex*-shoemakers."

Shui-lian laughed. She was deeply touched by her friend's loyalty and persistence.

"What do you say?" Pan-pan urged. "Let's give it a try."

Pan-pan's last words caused a stir inside Shui-lian, the same quivering anticipation she had felt when she stepped off the deck of her family's boat and onto the firm clay of the shore more than three months ago. On that chilly morning she had had such high hopes of starting a new page in her life with her friend. Jin-lin had given up on her dreams, but Shui-lian's new friend had stood by her since they had met that day in Bengbu. The question of where her loyalty should stand was so obvious, yet Shui-lian still was pulled toward the direction in which Jin-lin had decided to go.

"I think—" Shui-lian stopped, pondering her willingness to throw water on Pan-pan's enthusiasm. "I think you're right. I also think you're too young to have so many old expressions in your head."

"I'm so glad to hear that," Pan-pan said, beaming. "And I also have an idea."

"Do you really?" Shui-lian chuckled at the thought of what a chatterbox her friend had become.

"Why don't we go to her restaurant tomorrow morning to check the place out secretly, since Sun Ming is coming to get us in the afternoon?" Pan-pan asked cheerily. She stopped. "But I don't know where the place is, or what it's called."

"It's something like 'Old Style,' if I heard her correctly," Shui-lian answered. "And she did say it's nearby. Don't worry, we'll find it."

"Good. You see, already two heads are better than one. Wait! I'll bet Lao Feng can give us the directions. We can leave him a note and at the same time let him know we'll be away tomorrow for a little while."

"All right," Shui-lian said. I'll tell her tomorrow for sure, she thought.

PAN-PAN AND S\HUI-LIAN got up the next morning to find a note under a brick outside their tent. It gave them detailed instructions and a roughly sketched street map showing how to get to the restaurant, along with Lao Feng's blessings and wishes for good luck. They tiptoed past the house—needlessly, for the demolition crews had already begun to clatter and roar—and headed west. At the intersection designated by a star on Lao Feng's map, they turned north and walked three more blocks to

Sun Ming's street. A short distance east, they found themselves before a large residential compound filled with rows of high-rises. The area was bustling with early morning frenzy—pedestrians hurrying to and fro, and bikes, cars, and buses clogging the street. On the corner next to a bicycle parking lot stood a two-room brick building with a flat roof, above which the name *Lao Chuan Tong*—Old Tradition—was spelled out in neon. Sun Ming's restaurant. The left side seemed to be a fast-food dispensary, where a queue of people waited as fat steamed buns, freshly baked flat bread, and crispy deep-fried dough were handed out over the counter like batons in a relay race. The savoury aromas of fried meat and spring onions wafted over to Pan-pan and Shui-lian.

Making sure Sun Ming was nowhere in sight, Shui-lian took the lead across the road and stopped in front of the doorway to the restaurant's main room, where a curtain of sheer plastic strips allowed glimpses of the movement inside. The eating area of the restaurant, Shui-lian concluded. She stepped over to the window beside the door for a better look. A large blackboard filled with words and numbers covered the wall.

"It looks like a menu," Pan-pan whispered next to her. "My goodness, they're offering at least five dozen dishes. No wonder Sun Ming didn't want us to cook!"

"Look," Shui-lian hissed, pointing at a young woman passing by with a tray. Their eyes followed her, watching her put the tray down on a table occupied by two men and place a steaming bowl in front of each of them. Before she turned to leave, one man grabbed her sleeve and said something to her. The server burst out laughing.

"What's that all about?" Shui-lian murmured uneasily.

"Relax, Shui-lian. I'm not sure. This is a neighbourhood restaurant, so maybe they know each other. Not all men are bad, you know. Think about Lao Feng."

"I guess you're right," Shui-lian answered. "Anyway, I like what she's wearing."

"Pretty, isn't it?" Pan-pan agreed. "It's their uniform," she added, pointing at two other women who were shouting orders through the serving window at the back of the room. They wore bright yellow jackets in traditional style, with a mandarin collar and frog buttons across the upper chest and down the side under the arm.

"I wouldn't mind wearing one of those for a change," Shui-lian giggled, looking down at her threadbare shirt. "At Niavia we wore rags."

"So, what do you think?" Pan-pan asked. "It doesn't look too bad, does it?"

"Not at all. Now, you listen," Shui-lian scolded, mock seriously. "Stop sounding like an older sister. Remember, I'm older than you."

"How could I forget?"

THAT AFTERNOON, after a feast of Yangzhou fried rice, spicy stir-fried pork, and spinach served by one of the young women Shui-lian and Pan-pan had seen earlier, Sun Ming insisted the two girls head back to Lao Feng's place.

"You're my guests today. Tomorrow you begin work. That is, if you've decided to join me."

"We're looking forward to it," Shui-lian jumped in, eyeing Pan-pan, who smiled and nodded.

During the meal, Sun Ming had mentioned that Shui-lian and Pan-pan could move into a nearby apartment and live with four other women who worked for her. They were older but, like Pan-pan and Shui-lian, all came from other parts of the country. "You'll pay rent, like everyone else, but it's nominal," Sun Ming said, "and it would be better than living in a tent."

As soon as they arrived back at Lao Feng's house, Lao Feng wanted to hear their news, even before they had sat down. They told him about the delicious meal and Sun Ming's offer.

"Does that mean I can get a discount there?" he asked mischievously.

"You can always try," Pan-pan replied with the same lightheartedness. "One thing, though, we might learn how to cook someday and give you and Da-Ma a treat."

"But don't start to starve yourself right away," Shui-lian joked.

"You know what, Shui-lian? I'm so glad we came here, and happier still that we found Sun Ming. Every time I think about it, I can hardly believe such a miracle could happen."

Shui-lian looked at Pan-pan, whose face was lit up by a smile. "The real miracle," she said thoughtfully, "was finding a friend like you."

Pan-pan flushed and her eyes filled with tears. After she regained control of herself, she started talking with emotion. "After what happened today, especially what we saw in the restaurant, I couldn't help but wonder whether, if we work really hard there, someday you and I can open our own place. I even have a name for it already, *Shan Shui Fan Dian*—The Mountain and River Restaurant. What do you think?"

"How about The River and Mountain Restaurant? After all, I'm older."

The two friends burst out laughing.

"Whatever we call it," Shui-lian went on, "we'll make sure Lao Feng and Da-Ma will always get a big discount." She then grew serious. "But before we do anything like that, we should save up our money for you to see a doctor."

"Me? Doctor? What for?" Pan-pan frowned. "Oh, that," she said quietly, squeezing her arms against her ribs out of habit as she looked at the wall of bricks, a zigzagging silhouette across the ruined courtyard under the dim street light. The wall she and Shui-lian had built together.

"We'll see," she said.

Author's Note

Many readers may be surprised by the issue of "fox stink"—*hu chou*—in this story. In medical terms, fox stink is called axillary bromhidrosis.

There are two kinds of sweat glands in the human body: the eccrine glands, which secrete water and salt, and the apocrine, which release a milky fluid containing acids and fats. When broken down by bacteria, these acids and fats produce a noticeable odour—what North Americans call B.O. Different people produce different amounts of apocrine sweat; a few produce a lot. This condition is inherited.

In China there is a very strong cultural aversion to apocrine sweat odour. Deodorants and anti-perspirants like those commonly used in North America and Europe are not widely employed there.

During my latest trip to China (spring 2007) I saw various advertisements posted on buses, the walls of buildings, and electric poles by individuals, doctors, and even hospitals, offering to cure fox stink.

Acknowledgments

Mountain Girl, River Girl is a work of fiction, although the seeds of the story were planted by two young women whom Bill, my husband, and I met in a small restaurant on a quiet street off Changan Avenue in downtown Beijing. The modest restaurant was frequented largely by local residents and transient workers. One day Bill and I went there for breakfast. The two youngest servers were curious about the foreigner at one of their tables. They looked happy, and they giggled as they took our order. Each appeared not a day older than fifteen and spoke with a heavy Sichuan accent. I wondered what had brought them to the capital and a job in a restaurant. I couldn't help recalling my own youth nearly forty years ago when I lived in China, even though, unlike me and millions of others, they had not been forced by the government to leave their homes.

We returned to the restaurant a few times. But not until the last meal, when we were ushered into a special windowless room in the rear, did I have the chance to speak privately to the girls. They were fifteen years old, not eighteen as they had told us previously.

"My father wanted to get rid of me from the day I was born," one said quietly, while her friend, the shy one, said nothing but kept her eye on the doorway in case the boss came in. "He wanted a son. If it were not for my grandmother, I wouldn't have been kept alive. Grandma died a few years ago. I always knew that my mother would be allowed to have another baby only if I disappeared."

Bill and I continued our travels, but their words and images stayed with me throughout the trip. Before I left China three weeks later, I knew I would write a story inspired by the two girls from Sichuan.

Bill and I returned to China two years later with a group of friends. As soon as we arrived in Beijing, I went to the restaurant. It had the same sign above the entrance, the same door of stiff plastic strips that had yellowed with the passage of time. I stood at the doorway, seeking the two faces that had engraved themselves in my memory. I wondered if they would remember me. There were five young women busy serving and shouting orders toward the kitchen. I didn't recognize any of them. The owner of the restaurant was sitting in a corner facing the entrance. When she saw me walk toward her, she stood and headed toward the kitchen.

"Do you remember me?" I asked.

"Yes. What do you want?"

"I just want to know if the girls I met two years ago are still with you."

"They left a long time ago."

"Where did they go?" I asked, moving to the left so that I could peek into the kitchen, hoping to find them there.

"How do I know where they went? They've moved on, and that's that."

All I wanted was to tell the girls from Sichuan that I had written a book after I met them and to ask their names so that I could thank them properly. But they were gone.

My thanks go to my editor, Barbara Berson, for her thoughtful suggestions and comments, and to David Davidar for his warm welcome and support. To John Pearce, who is a friend and an agent equipped with a pencil and eraser. (The old trade dies hard.) To Ye Zhong-xing for the calligraphy that graces this book. To Judy Phillips for her skilful copy editing. Thanks are also due to the Ontario Arts Council and Canada Council for the Arts, for being there and for supporting this project.

I am grateful for having two wonderful brothers who have offered valuable suggestions and shared with me their past and present experiences. I am so sorry that years ago one of them spent two years working in a sweatshop in China.

Last but not least I want to thank Bill for always being with me. His love and encouragement as well as his fine expertise in words made this book possible.